MERICA

*The Diary
of Minnie Swift*

CHRISTMAS
AFTER ALL

KATHRYN LASKY

SCHOLASTIC INC. ✦ NEW YORK

IN MEMORY OF MY MOTHER,
HORTENSE FALENDER LASKY;
HER SISTERS AND BROTHER;
AND MY FATHER, MARVEN LASKY

Copyright © 2001 by Kathryn Lasky

All rights reserved. Published by Scholastic Inc., *Publishers since 1920*.
SCHOLASTIC, DEAR AMERICA, and associated logos are trademarks and/or registered
trademarks of Scholastic Inc. No part of this publication may be reproduced,
stored in a retrieval system, or transmitted in any form or by any means,
electronic, mechanical, photocopying, recording, or otherwise, without written
permission of the publisher. For information regarding permission, write to
Scholastic Inc., Attention: Permissions Department,
557 Broadway, New York, NY 10012.

The Library of Congress has cataloged the earlier hardcover edition as follows:
Lasky, Kathryn. Christmas after all : the diary of Minnie Swift / by Kathryn Lasky.
p. cm. — (Dear America) Summary: In her fictionalized journal, eleven-year-old Minnie
Swift recounts how her family dealt with the difficult times during the Depression and
how the arrival of an orphan from Texas changed their lives in Indianapolis just before
Christmas 1932. ISBN 0-439-21943-4 1. Depressions — 1929 — Juvenile fiction.
[1. Depressions — 1929 — Fiction. 2. Family life — Indiana — Fiction. 3. Orphans — Fiction.
4. Diaries — Fiction. 5. Indiana — Fiction.] I. Title. II. Series.
PZ7.L3274 Ch 2001 [Fic] — dc21 00-067031

This edition ISBN 978-0-545-38177-2

10 9 8 7 6 5 4 3 2 1   12 13 14 15 16

The text type was set in ITC Legacy Serif.
The display type was set in Horndon EF and AT Eccentric.
Book design by Kevin Callahan
Photo research by Amla Sanghvi

Printed in the U.S.A. 23
This edition first printing, September 2012

INDIANAPOLIS, INDIANA

1932

Mama and Papa believe in cold. That's why I tell Lady we have nothing to fear. You see, Mama and Papa have toughened us up on the sleeping porch. That's where we sleep with no heat and just screens, and not just in summer but all through the fall and beginning again in early spring. We're used to cold. But now we're going to be hardened off for the rest of the year in the rest of the house.

You see, Mama and Papa are closing off the dining room and the big library and four bedrooms. We are moving the dining table into the living room. Ozzie will sleep in what he calls his "lab," which is really a closet. Lady and I will be in his bedroom. It has all of Ozzie's favorite comic strips taped to the walls. Lady hates this. She has made the old bedroom that she and I share like a "boudoir." That's a French word for fancy dressing room. Lady loves Hollywood and fashion. And she sews really well. So our bedroom has pink satin bedspreads and this fluffy skirt around a dressing table and pictures of Lady's favorite movie stars on the wall. It might be glamorous, but it's too

3

expensive to heat. That's why we have to move into Ozzie's room, which is not a bit glamorous, and he swears that if we change a thing he'll murder us. Clem and Gwen's room is too hard to heat as well. So they will be in Mama's sewing room.

This is going to save us almost six dollars a month on coal and as Mama says, "We need every penny." That's because of the Depression. We aren't as bad off as most. Papa still has a job at Greenhandle Scrap Iron. He is their chief accountant. But there's not much to account for now. They used to be the biggest supplier of scrap iron and metal for the manufacture of automobiles in Indianapolis, but now so many places have closed.

Papa never talks about dollars or pennies or money. His eyes just seem dimmer every evening when he returns from work, and he seems to return a little earlier every evening.

This is going to be an odd Christmas, no doubt about it. Instead of sugar plums and stockings stuffed with goodies and stacks of presents under the tree—a Time of Bounty—I am thinking of this as The Time of the Dwindling. Everything is diminishing: our money, the light of day, and even the hours that Papa works. But in my heart I know we Swifts are tough—hardened off like seedlings. I just know that somehow, someway, this shall be a Christmas. Not the same kind of Christmas as others in the past, but maybe one to remember all the same. Must go. Almost time to listen to *Tarzan of the Apes.*

NOVEMBER 26, 1932

I came downstairs this morning and there is Mama in the kitchen in her fur coat and muffler with her hat on as it was so cold and she is standing over the hot air vent as still as a statue. The only thing that moves is a fluttering piece of yellow paper in her hands. A telegram. I get so nervous. So I blurt out, "Who died?"

"No one died, Minnie." She pauses. "But this is perplexing." Papa comes in with the newspaper. He sees Mama with the fluttering piece of yellow paper and says, "Who died?" And Mama says, "Yee gads." That's Mama's favorite expression—yee gads. "Nobody died, Sam. Quite the reverse."

Then at that very moment, Lady comes down the stairs with her long satin bathrobe trailing Jean Harlow–style. "Mama, are you having a baby?"

Mama blushes red right to the roots of her ashy brown hair. "Adelaide, please!" She calls Lady that when she's angry.

"Well, you said, 'quite the reverse.' So the opposite of dying is giving birth." Mama gives Lady a fierce look. Then she gives the telegram a shake, clears her throat, and begins to read: "No room for Willie Faye Darling in our jalopy. Heading west to California. Willie Faye on the Monon. Will arrive Union Station November 27, 5 P.M."

"Edwina and that fellow she married down in Texas—their daughter?" Papa whispers.

"Yes," Mama says. "That is surely where this telegram is from—Heart's Bend, Texas."

"Heart's Bend," Papa says as if he can't believe there is a town with such a strange name. "Willie Faye Darling?"

"Wilma Deering! Wilma Deering is coming here!" Ozzie whoops as he comes downstairs, still in his pajamas but with his winter coat on. "Wilma Deering—you mean Buck Rogers's girlfriend?" Ozzie's eyes are practically popping. His hair stands out all over his head like pale flames from a fire.

"No, idiot!" Lady says. "Buck's girlfriend is

6

Wilma Deering. Anyway, Willie Faye is real." She stops and adds, "Whoever she is."

Then about an hour later another longer telegram followed the first explaining that Willie Faye's parents had both died, her mother just last month, and that Willie Faye was eleven years old and an obedient child. When Mama read that, Lady said, "Oh, for Lord's sake, what a terrible thing to say about a person. I'd die if that were my epitaph."

"You'd already be dead if that were your epitaph," Clem told her. I thought that was pretty funny, but Mama told us all to be quiet. She had to think. While she was thinking, Ozzie moaned about another girl in the house and why couldn't it be an orphan boy. But I am happy that it is someone just my age, especially with me being the youngest girl. Lady is sixteen, Clementine is seventeen, and Gwendolyn is twenty.

NOVEMBER 27, 1932

"Willie Faye is real . . . whoever she is."

I cannot forget Lady's words. They were just words when she said them, but now they have become full of strange meaning. I guess Willie Faye is real but I have never in my life seen anything like her. And she's only been here three hours! Her train arrived on time at five o'clock, and now it's eight o'clock. And for the "whoever she is" part of Lady's words — well, she is our first cousin once removed or something like that, and she's an orphan! I never thought I would meet a real orphan. Ozzie said something "extremely insensitive," as Gwendolyn put it. When he found out she was an orphan, he said he thought orphans lived in special homes, and Mama said that they did, and Willie Faye was going to live with us in our home. I could have just killed Ozzie right on the spot. I mean, he's almost ten years old, he should know better, and to say it right in front of Willie Faye. For pity sakes! For someone who has been building crystal radios since he was seven, he should be smarter about other things. As Lady says, Ozzie has "no social skills, even if he can do logarithms."

LATER

I am writing this in bed with a flashlight. Willie Faye is sound asleep in the daybed Mama fixed up for her in the room with Lady and me. Guess what Willie Faye tried to do before we went to bed? She took a little jacket she had and began rolling it up real tight and went over to the bedroom window. When Lady and I asked her what she was doing, she said, "Don't you want to plug it up so no dust will blow in?" I guess that dust is practically all they have out there in Heart's Bend, Texas. Lady told her that she didn't have to bother, that there was not that kind of dust here in Indianapolis. She kind of blinked at us as if she could only half believe it. This wasn't the first time she blinked, either. I guess everything about us seems a little strange to Willie Faye. She didn't know what half those comic strips were that Ozzie had taped up. She had heard of Little Orphan Annie, but not Dick Tracy. She just loved Popeye. I explained about him and Sweet Pea the baby and Olive Oyl and her nasty brother Castor Oyl. She got that joke. But she'd never heard of Buck Rogers. Ozzie had a strip with Buck and Wilma clinging with magnetic grapplers to a spaceship and Willie Faye just didn't get it. "Spaceship?" she said. "Is there such a thing?" I had to explain how Buck Rogers is science fiction that takes place in the twenty-fifth century. This just flummoxed Willie Faye. "Twenty-fifth century!" she kept saying. "Who can imagine the twenty-fifth century?" I could almost see her trying to count the years in her head. She's a strange little thing. But just think! Never having heard of Popeye or Buck Rogers. And that wasn't all she hadn't heard of—it's unbelievable.

ALMOST MIDNIGHT

Can't fall asleep. Too much to think about. This has been a very weird day, starting at five o'clock this afternoon when we met Willie Faye's train. It's Gwendolyn who helped Mama figure stuff out about where Willie Faye would sleep and how to arrange the extra bed. Gwendolyn's boyfriend, Delbert Frink—yes, that is his name and he is as weird as his name, in Lady's and my opinion—came over and helped Papa move the daybed upstairs. Mama coached them around corners. Lady, Ozzie, and I nearly threw up as Mama kept praising Delbert. "Oh, Delbert Frink, you are a wonder! Oh, Delbert this and Delbert that." It was "nauseating," as Lady says. Delbert wears much too much hair oil and he even speaks in any oily way. The words kind of ooze out of him, high and squeaky as if they are coming through his nose.

Anyway, this afternoon we all went down to meet Willie Faye at Union Station. We took the Packard and Delbert drove his Duesenberg. Between the two automobiles we all could go.

I hear Mama on the stairs now. Must stop.

TWENTY MINUTES LATER

Phew! She's gone to bed. I can write again. I'm a little bit worried. That's probably why I can't sleep. Tomorrow's Monday. I have to take Willie Faye to school with me. I go to 70. That's public school number 70. All of us Swift children have gone there. It's an elementary school. I'm just hoping at 70 they will let Willie Faye into sixth grade when they see her. I mean, she is teensy. And I don't think she knows the first thing about long

11

division and we're about to start on decimals.

Lady goes to an all-girls' private school called Tudor Hall because Mama and Papa feel she is "distractible." Clem goes to Shortridge, the public high school. It's huge and they have lockers. I can't imagine myself going to Shortridge in three years. You could fit two Willie Fayes in one Shortridge locker. It's not all girls, though. There are lots of boys. Cute ones, not like Delbert Frink, but so far Clem doesn't have a boyfriend. She has two best girl pals. We call them the O's, because one is named Olive and the other Opal. Clem and the O's are very serious. They study a lot and belong to the social service club. Olive is the president of the club. Lady says coeducation is utterly wasted on them. They have never been to a prom. They never go on dates.

Tudor Hall has proms and Lady goes to them. She went last year with a boy she couldn't stand but she had made a lovely dress and wanted to wear it. Lady is quite handy with a needle and thread. Mama says she truly could turn a sow's ear into a silk purse. Shoot! Mama just snuck in and told me to turn off the flashlight. I'm going to wake up later and write the rest. . . .

AFTER MIDNIGHT

I'm good at waking up. I never need an alarm clock. Anyway, I have to finish telling about Willie Faye. I have to sort it all out in my mind. It's not that Willie Faye is complicated, she is just so different. I could tell that everyone thought so. Even Clem, and nothing ever throws Clem, but Willie Faye does. As I said, Willie Faye is teeny, teeny but she's my age. In fact two months older! But she doesn't look like any sixth grader I've ever seen. She looks about like a fourth grader or maybe even a third grader. Those dust storms that they are always talking about out west — well, Willie Faye looks like she was blown in by those scouring winds. We nearly missed her. She was on the platform standing in the shadow of a big pillar with her cardboard suitcase nearly half as big as she is and holding a basket. Her hair seemed to blow about her head as if it were in its own private storm, but it was really just sticking out stiff with grit. Her wool stockings were falling down and her shoes had busted at the seams, but I didn't notice that until later. I was looking at this little face peeking out of the basket. It was a cat. She saw me looking at the cat. And then she spoke. This very old-sounding voice came out of this little body. "He's a miracle, all right," she said, looking at the kitty. "Tumbleweed is a downright miracle."

Mama leaned over and said in kind of a questioning voice, "Willie Faye? Willie Faye Darling?" She nodded yes. Mama had to almost get down on her knees to be eye level with her. She said, "I'm your cousin Belle Swift," and then she gave her a kiss on the cheek. And guess what? There was a big blotch left on Willie Faye's cheek where Mama's lips had blotted up the dust. And when Mama stood up there was a streak of dust on her own chin.

Then that little old voice again. "Hope you don't mind, ma'am, that I brought my cat. But if I'd left him he'd have just smothered to death." Next she said something that almost made my drawers drop. "I had to suck out his nose every morning, noon, and night. He was about the only cat left in the whole Texas Panhandle." Imagine sucking out a cat's nostrils! That's the limit. I like cats but I'm not sure if I like them that much.

Anyway, when we started walking I noticed these little clouds of dark dust puffing out of her shoes. And then when we got home Mama said that I should go up and help Willie Faye draw a bath. So I took her into the bathroom and she just stopped dead in her tracks. So I say, "What's wrong?" And she says, "What is this?" She was blinking in disbelief.

"It's a bathroom," I say.

"Is that the pot?" She points at the toilet. And I say yes. Well, this was the first bathroom Willie Faye had ever seen. Back in Heart's Bend she bathed in an old tin washtub, and they went to an outhouse to do their business and had to pump water from a well. I'm not sure if she's ever seen a water faucet. Is that unbelievable?

Anyway, I drew the bath for her and I even let her use some of my bubble bath. After a while I heard the water draining out of the tub. Then it seemed like forever but Willie Faye was still in there. So I called in and she said in a kind of scared voice, "Oh, I'm just trying to clean the tub." So I said I would help her. She seemed slow to answer and then I thought I heard her crying. So I pushed the door open a bit. Well, that tub was nearly black with dirt. "I guess I'm pretty dirty," she said. "Maybe too dirty to be in such a nice house. I think I've ruined your tub." I felt so sorry for her. So I just went downstairs and got the 20 Mule Team Borax cleaning powder. We got it all cleaned up and the tub looked as white and bright as ever.

She only had one change of underwear in her suitcase but we found some old underpants and socks of mine for her. As a matter of fact she hardly had anything in her suitcase. When I asked her if she was having more stuff sent, she said no, that is all she owns. So here is what Willie Faye owns: two pairs of underpants, one pair of socks, two undershirts, the dress she was wearing, a sweater, a coat, a cigar box full of colored pencils, a little book to draw in, and a picture from a newspaper. The picture is of Willie Faye standing by the biggest pumpkin you ever saw. Over the picture it says "Littlest Girl Grows Biggest Pumpkin." She grew it all by herself. She said she'd tell me the story about it someday. But she did show me some of the pumpkin seeds that she brought from it. She said we could try to plant them come spring.

P.S. Forgot to say that Willie Faye's sweater was made from this rough material and I said to her

I had never seen wool like that. She just laughed and said it wasn't wool at all. It was made from an old feed bag. I wasn't sure what she meant, and she told me feed bags were the burlap bags that grain and stuff came in that they fed to their chickens! Can you beat that?

NOVEMBER 20, 1932 — JUST AFTER SCHOOL

This is so awful! I just can't believe this is happening. They put Willie Faye in the fourth grade! She's not that dumb. This is so embarrassing. I can't stand it. Miss Cuddy said that it has nothing to do with Willie Faye but with the schools she attended. They "obviously weren't up to snuff." It's true that she doesn't know a fraction from a blue jay. And her handwriting is very wobbly. She had never even heard of having to practice drawing ovals on a slant to develop the proper way of writing script. And she only knew a few state capitals. Her reading is pretty good, though. Miss Cuddy thought it might be too "stressful" for her in a higher grade. Well, I'll tell you who has stress. Me! What am I going to do on the playground? Hang around with a bunch of fourth graders? I'll never live this down.

Martine Vontill, that snot-nosed stuck-up thing, was already rubbing it in about my "little half-educated cousin." Then in her usual pushy way she started battering poor Willie Faye with questions. Where'd you get those shoes? How come you're so little? Why do you talk funny?

"A charming child," as Lady would say. The boys hardly paid any attention to Willie Faye, but my two best friends Lucy Meyers and Betty Hodges were really nice.

Betty and Lucy and I were invited last week to Bernadette Otis's birthday party, and I'm not quite sure how to ask her if Willie Faye can come. I mean, if it were Lucy or Betty I wouldn't feel funny, but I don't know Bernadette as well. She and Martine are best friends, but she's not snotty like Martine. Of course she lets Martine boss her around all the time.

Funny thing is, none of this fourth-grade business or Martine's snottiness seemed to bother Willie Faye. She worried most that Tumbleweed would miss her when she went to school. Lady said Willie Faye shouldn't worry — "cats aren't that deep." But I'm not sure if Lady's right. A cat has thirty-two muscles in each ear. That's a fact.

Ozzie told me. He knows all sorts of stuff like that. How shallow can you be with thirty-two muscles in each ear? You must pick up on a lot. We weren't sure if Willie Faye could even go to school with me this morning because it had snowed and her shoes were falling apart. Her feet are so small. Everyone passes her shoes down to me because I have the smallest feet in the family. Gwen being the oldest and Ozzie being the only boy are the only ones who ever get new shoes, or at least in the last few years since times have been so bad. Well, Willie Faye's feet are too small for any of my shoes, but then Ozzie went into his lab and found some electrical tape that he uses for patching together his inventions and we taped up her shoes.

They made us go outside during recess, which I thought was rotten. It was snowing harder and was only twenty-two degrees on the thermometer outside our classroom window. I asked Miss Loritz, who was on playground duty, if we could be excused and stay in because of the sorry state of Willie Faye's shoes. I thought this would save me from having to hang around with the fourth graders. Miss Loritz said that Willie Faye could stay in and help her wash the blackboards but that

I had to go out. Willie Faye said she'd rather go outside with me.

They won't let us play in the park anymore because they say there are too many hobos. We have to stay in the playground because those hobos drift over from Curtisville Bottom. That's Indianapolis's shantytown where all the bums and really poor people who have lost their jobs during the Depression live. Most other places call them Hoovervilles after President Herbert Hoover. But we call ours after his vice president, Charles Curtis. Lady thinks it's second-rate that we don't call ours after the president. I never even knew the president's first name was Herbert because Papa always called him That Fool Hoover. I thought for the longest time his name was Thatfull Hoover. Anyhow, we went outside and shivered but then Henry Thatcher started a snowball fight, and I don't know why but somehow Ozzie got into the thick of it and we were all making and throwing snowballs. Willie Faye actually is quite good despite her size. So we were all getting nice and warmed up when Miss Gordon, the principal, came out and rang the bell for us all to come in.

This is funny. Willie Faye has only seen snow

twice in her life. She said once there was so much of it that she would have been glad to never see it again. There are many things that Willie Faye has never seen, like a toilet and a porcelain bathtub. I might start making a list.

LATER

I finished my homework and helped Willie Faye with hers. Gwen helped, too. We're getting her "up to snuff," as Gwen says, in spelling and grammar. I couldn't believe it but Willie Faye did not know what an adjective was. I never heard of such a thing. We're starting to diagram sentences in the sixth grade. I don't know how she will ever learn to do that without knowing what an adjective is. Well, she knows now. But how can a person spend eleven years on God's green earth and not know what an adjective is? Our words for spelling in my class are mostly Christmas words—"wreath," "angel" (and then to be tricky, "angle"), "nativity," stuff like that. And then there is always a surprise word from the "hard list" that we are supposed to study each week. In the fourth grade they have a lot of Christmas words, too. There is one thing, however, that Willie Faye is up to snuff in. She draws really well.

Whoops! Have to stop writing. Mama just announced that we are going to Stout's Shoe Store to buy Willie Faye a new pair of shoes. This is the best thing that's happened all day. I love Stout's Shoe Store. Of course it is sort of hard going when you know that you won't be the one to get new shoes. But Ozzie and I love playing with the fluoroscope. You stand up on a small staircase and stick your feet under this big machine and look in through something that's kind of like binoculars, and you get to see the bones of your feet and you can wriggle your toes and see those toe bones jiggle around. It's the greatest. Next to going to the picture show, doing the fluoroscope is my favorite activity.

JUST BEFORE DINNER

We're back from Stout's. It really is the cat's whiskers as far as shoe stores go. Willie Faye couldn't believe the place. When you walk into Stout's the first thing you see is this big old parrot—a real live parrot from the Amazon jungle. It's green and blue with a touch of yellow. And sometimes it squawks hello and sometimes it says, "Get away from my cage." It's generally pretty rude. It did say "Merry Christmas" today and there was a big red bow on its cage. Well, Willie Faye nearly popped her eyes on that. Stout's carries Polly Parrot shoes for children, so that is why they have the parrot. Kind of like an advertisement.

So then we go in and Mama talks to young Mr. Stout about what Willie Faye needs, and they bring out the Brannock — that's the metal thing you step on so they can measure your feet. Ozzie and I go off to mess with the fluoroscope. I can see Willie Faye looking overhead at the baskets whizzing on the wires. That's how they do business at Stout's. When you decide on a pair of shoes you take your money to a counter. They put it in a little box and send it up with the shoes in a basket to the mezzanine. Then they wrap the shoes in brown paper and send them in a bag with your change back to another counter, the pickup counter. We watched Willie Faye's shoes come back all wrapped up in brown paper. She didn't want to wear them home. She didn't get Polly Parrots. She got Buster Brown oxfords because Mama felt they were sturdier even though they did cost more. Mama had a very serious expression on her face when she took out those four one-dollar bills. And then when we were coming home we passed a new soup kitchen where the city gives out free bread and food, usually soup, to people. The line was very long. It went around the corner. Mama just looked straight ahead. I know what she was thinking about — those four dollars that she had just spent on the shoes for Willie Faye and how pathetic the people in the soup line looked. Some were sitting down on the sidewalk with newspapers spread over their shoulders and knees for warmth. Lady told me that they call those Hoover blankets. Well, at least they haven't started calling them Curtis blankets here in Indianapolis.

P.S. We were surprised when we got home from Stout's that Papa was already home. He was up in his little attic room where he sometimes goes when he brings work home from the office. He keeps an adding machine and an old typewriter up there. I hear the k-chirp sound of the typewriter more than the k-chung of the adding machine lately.

My fingers are tired from poking cloves into oranges. So I'm going to write in my diary until *Charlie Chan* comes on. We've all been making pomander balls for Christmas presents, but it does wear out the fingers. Willie Faye had never made one and Gwen says she is naturally artistic because she stuck in the cloves in a spiral pattern. Everyone is making them except for Lady, of course, who has decided to turn her old prom dress into curtains and is stitching on them. Dumbest thing I ever heard of and she wants to hang them up in our room. She saw a picture in a magazine of Jean Harlow the movie star's boudoir and she had these filmy curtains in what they called "kidney-shaped drapery" and Lady thinks they would just be the cat's whiskers in our bedroom. I say, who wants kidneys hanging from their windows?

"It's very Hollywood," says Lady.

"It's kidneys," says Clem.

"Girls!" says Mama.

"Kidneys," says Ozzie, "make urine. You have pee pee curtains. In my old bedroom! They should be yellow." Ozzie, Willie Faye, and I just howl. Mama says, "Francis Osgood Swift!"

We all shut up.

LATER

Mama looked up from her sewing and said, "Ozzie, turn on the Spartan." I could see that Willie Faye didn't know what on God's green earth she was talking about, until Ozzie got up and turned on the radio. We have a Sparks Worthington Spartan 31. Ozzie says it is the best radio made today. We bought it a couple of years ago when business was better at Greenhandle's. Lady says it looks like a tombstone. But Gwen says it looks like a beautiful French cathedral—like Notre Dame in Paris, France. Gwen has been to Paris to study. She went two years ago with a group of students from Wellesley College, the school she went to outside of Boston. She couldn't go back this year because we couldn't afford the tuition. So now she works at the Bobbs-Merrill publishing company here in Indianapolis. She doesn't mind that much because she gets to meet a lot of writers and Gwen dreams of becoming a writer. Anyhow, I think the Spartan is just plain beautiful. It stands nearly a foot tall on the table. Its dark amber-colored wood just gleams. The speaker screen through which the voices come out is shaped like the fantail of a peacock with thin curved ribs of wood between the sections. But the best part is the dial. It has what they call a shadow projection. There is a little halo of honey-colored light around it and the pointer works like a shadow when you move it through the arc to the different stations.

Heavens, they are starting to play the Esso Gasoline music. Papa isn't down yet from his room. Esso Gasoline and Motor Lube is the sponsor of the show. Papa usually is here early for *Charlie Chan* and he didn't come down for the six o'clock news, either, and they were talking all about President-elect Roosevelt and his New Deal, which is supposed to help end the Depression. Next to their children I think Mama and Papa love Franklin and Eleanor Roosevelt the most. They are crazy nuts for Mr. FDR.

It's snowing really hard now outside and the windows are getting all lacy with frost. Tumbleweed has settled near the heating vent and I swear little puffs of dust are coming up from his fur. Clementine said that she heard that a good way to bathe a cat, because Lord knows you can't really bathe them with water, is to brush them with a mixture of baby powder and baking soda. Willie Faye looks as if she's not too sure.

STILL LATER

I hated supper tonight. It was meatless meat loaf. I think we should just call it weird loaf. It has everything but meat in it—peanuts, cottage cheese, rice. It's cheap. We hardly ever have meat anymore, except for chicken, because we raise them in the garage. But we only have chicken maybe once a month or so at the most. The other disgusting thing we always are having is O'Grotons. O'Grotons means you put cheese and flour in everything to thicken it up and then stretch it out. So we have something like hot dog and potatoes O'Groton and Mama puts just about two hot dogs all cut up in the whole thing and a bunch of potatoes and then stretches it with the cheese. It's vile. But we are not allowed to say anything bad about food. This riles Mama and Papa like nothing else. We can get a real punishment for it—like being sent away from the table or not allowed to go out or something. They say there are too many starving families in these days of the Great Depression and we better darn well eat what is put in front of us or just shut up. Mama actually said the words "shut up" when I complained a while back about the cabbage O'Groton. I had never heard her say that before in my life. She is very gentle-spoken except when it comes to food.

Charlie Chan was good tonight. And that's another thing that Willie Faye had never heard about — the great Chinese detective. Except he's half-Chinese and half-Hawaiian so that means he's really American, even though Hawaii is only a territory. I had that argument with snot-nosed Martine Vontill. Anyhow, it was a murder tonight on the show but there was no body! And guess what? A parrot that Willie Faye and I agreed must look just like the one at Stout's was the main witness. It squawked out, "Murder, bloody murder!" Charlie has two sons, Number One Son and Number Two Son. Number One botched up good. And guess what Charlie said about him? "Sometimes quickest way to brain of young sprout is by impression on other end." Papa laughed, he really laughed. We haven't heard

Papa laugh in weeks, maybe months. And you should have seen Mama's face when he laughed. She just beamed. I swear if she had been sitting by the windowpane all the frost would have melted.

NOVEMBER 30, 1932

Jackie came back today and was in the kitchen when Willie Faye and I came down for breakfast. I don't know who was more shocked, Jackie or Willie Faye. I'm not sure if Willie Faye had ever seen a colored person before, at least one as big as Jackie, and I don't think Jackie had ever seen an eleven-year-old as teensy-weensy as Willie Faye. They just plain stared at each other for a good ten seconds. Jackie is our housemaid. She helps Mama cook and clean and she kills the chickens we keep in the coops in the garage. Jackie is the one who got us started on chickens. She has a cousin south of the city who raises them, and then she started herself and now she has all kinds of chickens: brown leghorns, white leghorns, Rhode Island Reds, barred rock bantams, wyandottes. Mama and Papa can't really afford to pay her much anymore so instead we give her food and all our old clothes, but she keeps bringing us chickens. Jackie says no sense looking for a job anywhere else. She's been here too long and is too old to change.

She was down in the southern part of the state at a funeral. Mama said that she hoped Jackie wouldn't show us pictures, like last time, of the dead person all laid out in the coffin. But Ozzie and I hope she will. She goes to a lot of funerals. And every time she comes back from one she seems to bring a couple of chickens with her. She has a soft spot for chickens, at least until she kills them.

Mama called Bernadette's mother about the birthday party and it is fine for Willie Faye to come. But when she hung up she just shook her head kind of sadlike. I asked what was wrong. And she just said she thought Mrs. Otis was worried about Mr. Otis. Then Lady said she had seen Mr. Otis selling apples at the corner of New York Street and Meridian by University Park. Mama just gasped and said, "Don't tell your father." Mama went absolutely white. And just last night she was beaming and shiny enough to melt the frost. I don't like these times. I don't care whether it's Christmas or not. There's something kind of scary going on.

LATER

I got bored in geography today and started making a list of all the things that Willie Faye has never heard of. Here it is:

Porcelain bathtubs
Toilets
Charlie Chan
Jean Harlow
Adjectives
Buck Rogers
Popeye
Dick Tracy

Papa is back early again. I'm hearing more k-chirp than k-chung from up there. Lady thinks that he is writing to apply for new jobs.

Willie Faye told us the story of her and that pumpkin. That pumpkin weighed over two hundred pounds and Willie Faye grew it all by herself. The pumpkin-growing part was interesting but not nearly so much as the rest of the story. She grew it by feeding it pans full of milk. Yes indeed! She told me that when a pumpkin's vine gets to a certain thickness you can notch it and then kind of push it down into a pan of milk. It will sop up the milk and it makes it grow like crazy. This is unbelievable but a pumpkin can grow between four and six inches in just twelve hours. Its main growing time is between seven in the evening and seven in the morning. Willie Faye's pumpkin grew so big that they had to borrow a neighbor's truck to take it to the fair in some town called Amarillo.

When they brought it back from the fair, Willie Faye's mother said pumpkins that big lacked in flavor and there wasn't much you could do with them. So her father was going to chop it up and feed it to the hogs. But then Willie Faye said before he did that could he chop a little door and a window in it, and hollow it out a bit. She had always wanted a playhouse in a pumpkin! Now, isn't that the keenest idea? So he did. He had to use a big saw to do it. She said it was kind of sticky playing inside, but really lovely at sunset. She had the door and window facing west and she said when the sun streamed through, it turned everything gold inside. Even her skin looked gold and shimmery.

Ozzie said the funniest thing. He said that she should have put wheels on it, then gotten those pigs to carry her to a ball like Cinderella when she went and met her Prince Charming. Well, we all just howled at that. But then Willie Faye told us what finally happened to her pumpkin house. It started to get kind of soft around the edges from squatting in that hot Texas sun, and she reckoned — this must be a western word, Willie Faye always says "reckon" — that it would start to cave in and that she would have just a few more days of playing in it. So one morning after a cold night she went out to the pumpkin house. She crawled in and she said she just froze. There was a whole mess of rattlesnakes. Lucky for her they were still kind of drowsy. But then one of them woke up. He coiled up on top of the heap of other snakes and reared his head like he was about to strike. Willie Faye backed right out of that pumpkin house!

And this was not her first meeting up with rattlesnakes. Her daddy got bit by a snake once and her mother had to carve an *X* with a big sharp knife right in the bite and suck out the venom.

Willie Faye is a very interesting person. She may not know about some things, but she's got a whole mess of other stuff that she knows about and she tells it all very fine.

. . .

P.S. Guess what? There is something I didn't know about — O'Groton. It's not spelled that way. It's spelled au gratin, which means "with cheese" in French. It doesn't make it taste any better. We had cauliflower au gratin tonight and it was still vomitous. A good eight on the vomitron. Ozzie and I have invented the vomitometric scale, or for short the vomitron and it goes from zero to ten.

DECEMBER 1, 1932

When we came back from school today we smelled all sorts of good things. Mama and Jackie were baking cookies for Mama's literary club. Mama belongs to two ladies' clubs, the Indianapolis Woman's Club and the Fortnightly Club — one eats and the other doesn't. As far as I can see that is the main difference. It's just about all the same ladies in both clubs, but in one they talk about books and in the other they write papers about boring things. In the Woman's Club all they serve is ice water! I would never belong to such a club. Ice water and highfalutin intellectual ideas. Enough to make you throw up even without any food.

Jackie makes little dough folk for me and Willie

Faye and Ozzie. Ozzie drips green food coloring on his so it will look like a Martian. Then Jackie says, "How you know a Martian's green, Oz?"

This begins one of Ozzie and Jackie's long arguments.

Ozzie says something about how in space there is no atmosphere and no oxygen. "But he ain't in space, he's on Mars," Jackie argues.

"That's just the point," says Ozzie. He believes that on Mars there are chlorophyll beings and that they are kind of like plants — they breathe carbon dioxide. And then Jackie says, "Well, maybe there be colored beings up there. Not green but black and brown and cinnamon color like me." Jackie is kind of the color of cinnamon. So on and on they go, round and round in circles. One thing is for sure: Ozzie is absolutely certain that there is life out there in space on some planet. He calls them extraterrestrial life forms. Ozzie's biggest ambition in life is to build a kind of immense ear that can listen for signals from space. But in the meantime he's working on a homemade telephone, which I guess is a kind of ear as well as a mouth.

Mama gave us fifty cents to go to Nick Kerz to buy a birthday present for Bernadette. Nick Kerz is the limit as far as toy stores go, although on the first floor they have what they call notions and things that aren't toys at all, like thread and thimbles and yardsticks. Very boring stuff. We walked there. Willie Faye couldn't believe her eyes. Floor to ceiling toys—dolls, dollhouse stuff, board games, puppets, whirligigs, toy cars, trucks. All that was too expensive. We bought Bernadette a set of jacks and a ball and then down in the notions department we got her a Christmas hair bow.

This weekend Santa Claus comes to Nick Kerz. It's really Mr. Jones, a relative of the owner, who dresses up. The little kids sit on his lap and then they look around and point to the things they want for Christmas.

LATER

We took the long way home. Here's something else Willie Faye didn't know about. Booth Tarkington. He's only the most famous author in America, maybe the world, for all I know, and he lives on our street—yes, just four blocks down from us at 4270 North Meridian and our house is at 4605. Mama and Mrs. Tarkington both belong to the

Fortnightly Club. They call each other by their first names. She calls Mama Belle and Mama calls her Susanah.

Willie Faye has heard of Al Capone. Ozzie is almost as fascinated with Al Capone as he is with Martians. He was very disappointed that the law finally caught up with the famous gangster just for cheating on his taxes and not for murder. Papa says as long as the fiend is behind bars it's okay with him and he doesn't care if he's jailed for cheating at tiddlywinks. We need a new tiddlywinks set, by the way. We've lost all of our pieces. But it was too expensive at Nick Kerz—seventy-five cents!

AFTER SUPPER

Thank heavens Jackie is back from her funeral trip. Now we can eat decent. Supper was really good tonight. If I had had to have turkey marrow soup or turkey anything one more time I would have up and died. Not only that but Gwen likes to try to cook these recipes that she had to type out for the cookbook Bobbs-Merrill published called *Joy of Cooking*. Lady and I call it the *Sadness of Aspic*. Aspics are about the sorriest food a person

38

can encounter, in my opinion. They aren't exactly Jell-O and they aren't exactly pudding. But they are made into fancy molds and shake like a fat lady's behind. They are considered quite elegant. We have had tomato aspic, tongue aspic (cow tongue, as if one could make that meat any more disgusting than it already is), we have had vegetable juice aspic and a cucumber salad one. Mama says they are elegant and thrifty. I think they are vomitous. Aspic is a solid ten on the vomitron.

Ozzie and I almost threw up after the tongue aspic. We kind of wish we had. At least that would have proved our point. Ozzie said it would have been the cat's whiskers if we could have had a puke-athon. Nobody would have ever served aspic in this house again, that's for sure.

There's going to be one of those dance marathons starting on New Year's Eve. The idea is that couples dance all day and all night long with only a few minutes' break every hour to eat or go to the bathroom. The couple that dances the longest wins a pot of money. Some couples have danced as long as a month. Mama forbids us to go see them. She says that it's immoral and that people should not be forced to abuse their bodies in this kind of entertainment. Mama says the only person who should attend such a sorry spectacle is That Fool Hoover — he's the cause of it.

Tonight for supper we had turnip greens, corn-bread, and hash with Jackie's homemade catsup. The only good thing was dessert: chocolate pudding. Mama added that to make up for the rest of the dinner.

Mama says that Willie Faye and I should go over our spelling words one more time since the test is tomorrow. Clem has to have Ozzie help her with her physics homework. Willie Faye at first didn't understand how a nine-year-old in the fifth grade could help a seventeen-year-old in the twelfth grade. But I think she is beginning to. We went into Ozzie's lab. He showed her his crystal radio and let her use the headphones. She got a funny look on her face.

"What's on?" Ozzie asked and he took the ear-phones for a second. "Ooh!" Ozzie made a face. "Rudy Vallee." Ozzie and I purely hate Rudy Vallee. He's this stupid singer. He was singing "Love Letters in the Sand." A nine on the vomitron — just behind aspic.

Ozzie explains to Willie Faye all about crystal radios and how he builds them. He shows her a crystal — a galena crystal. They're the best, Ozzie says. They cost about four or five cents. He explains how these crystals are able to detect radio signals, for some strange reason, because of the minerals in them. The detection happens at a point between one of the crystals and the tip of a piece of wire. They call these wires cat's whiskers. That's why Ozzie is always saying "That's the cat's." Most people say, That's the cat's whiskers, or That's the cat's pajama's, meaning something is really good. Ozzie means it, too, when he says it but he is also thinking about crystal radios. His workbench is covered with wire and these things he calls capacitors and little coils.

DECEMBER 2, 1932

I'm so mad. I can't believe it. I missed two words on the spelling test. And Willie Faye got 100 on hers! I missed the word "nativity." That was just a silly mistake. I left out one *i*. But the other word was the surprise word "chrysanthemum." I mean, why would Miss Cuddy choose a big old fat springtime flower word from the surprise list on the second day in December, just going into the Christmas season?

I feel positively rotten. And to make matters worse Papa came in the door on our heels and said that the Hoosier Bank and Trust just closed. "Oh, Sam!" That's all Mama can ever say these days. He went straight up to his room. I think I'll go straight up to mine. I'm so tired I could drop. Willie Faye and I stayed up really late. More about that later. Willie Faye wants to go with Jackie to the garage and help her catch a chicken to kill. At least that's good: chicken for dinner. Oh, yes, and at least it's Friday. Only two more weeks of school before we get out for Christmas vacation.

AFTER NAP

I feel better. I don't ever want to hear or see the word "chrysanthemum" again, though. And I'll never grow those flowers. When I opened my eyes Willie Faye was sitting cross-legged on her bed and poking a wire through a feather. "What in creation are you doing?" I asked. Turns out she is making a Christmas present for Lady out of chicken feathers and some of Ozzie's copper wire that she begged off him. They are going to be earrings. And guess what: They will go perfectly with Lady's feather boa, the one she wore to the prom with the dress that has now been turned into a kidney-shaped curtain. I shall say it again: Willie Faye may not have known about toilets and bathtubs and adjectives, but by gum, I think she could be an inventor. I wonder if she'll make something for me for Christmas. I hope so. I was kind of cranky coming home from school about the spelling test and all. I think I'll try to make up to her now. I think she needs to know about the burden of my name — Minnie, short for Minerva. Yes indeed. My true name is Minerva Swift. Just think of that — Minerva, named for the goddess of wisdom. There's always this pressure, you see, to be smart. Not simply act smart, be smart. It is too much of a name for any mortal.

BEFORE SUPPER

I explained to Willie Faye about the name and all. She seemed to understand. One of the reasons I was so tired is that Willie Faye and I stayed up really late last night. First we got up after we should have been in bed and crept into Ozzie's lab. He has another set of earphones and the three of us traded them around and we listened to the *Texaco Star Theater* with Ed Wynn. It was easy to do with no one finding out. Everyone was downstairs listening to the same program on the Spartan, but it's on after our bedtime. And this is the funniest show ever. Here was one funny thing Ed Wynn said. He was talking about the opera *Carmen* and he said the lady who played the role was skinny. "Skinny as a bone," he said. "In fact she is so thin her own dog buried her three times in one week!" We had to laugh with our hands pressed over our mouths, but we heard them roaring downstairs—except for Papa. He was up in his room and we could hear the adding machine tonight—k-chung!

AFTER SUPPER

When Willie Faye and I went downstairs to set the table and help Jackie in the kitchen, guess who came knocking at the door? Onesy. Onesy is short for One and he is the only hobo that we allow in the kitchen. We call him Onesy because he has just one eye and one tooth, and he's missing a finger. So it kind of fits. He's nice, but he did smell a bit rank. So Jackie gave him a dishpan of hot water and another kettle full and told him to wash up before he sat down at her kitchen table. The chicken was just coming out of the oven and she gave him some grits left over from breakfast, and some pickled watermelon she had put up last summer, and tapioca. Tumbleweed seemed to like Onesy a lot. We're going to try the baby powder–baking soda mix on Tumbleweed this weekend.

Onesy told us he wants to marry Kate Smith. She's a lovely lady singer on the radio but I don't know how she would take to Onesy. I want Mama to get her hair fixed like Kate Smith's, but Lady says Mama's face is too narrow. She'd look like a pinhead with it all flat on the sides and then those little ridges waving back from her forehead. They call them finger waves. Lady says they'll be out of fashion by next year anyway. Lady really does know a lot about fashion.

Lady, Gwen, and Clem are all going out tonight with their gangs. Well, Gwen will go out with The Frink, as Lady and I call him. Lady is going out with a mystery man. She says she's going down to the Lyric Theater to meet the girls. But there are usually some boys and there has been one boy calling up here a lot lately. Clem is going out with Homer Peet, which is okay except I think he is totally in love with Clementine and when he is around her he is nearly speechless and drooling like a puppy. I really don't think Clem gives a hoo-ha about him. She just likes to go to the picture shows. Mama says she'll take Ozzie and me and Willie Faye to the picture shows tomorrow night after Bernadette's party if Ozzie and I won't argue about which picture show.

You see, we haven't been driving the Packard much lately to save on gas. Gas is ten cents a gallon and that is the same price as a picture show. So we have our picture show jelly jar and it really is filling with dimes saved from not driving the Packard.

In the meantime before *Buck Rogers* comes on the radio we go up and watch Lady put on her makeup. She's finally got her eyebrows plucked right so she doesn't have to use so much eyebrow pencil. She was practically bald up there this summer. She sits in front of the vanity in our bedroom and scootches up her lips and then draws first with red pencil around them. She directs most of her comments to Willie Faye because she knows I've heard it all. Willie Faye's eyes are glued to Lady. She has never even seen mascara, and she watches as Lady wets the little brush and brushes the black on her eyelashes. It really does transform her eyes. Ozzie comes in and makes a rude noise. He loves to annoy the girls when they are getting dressed up.

The doorbell rings. "The Frink," Lady and I say at once. Delbert always comes early.

"Time for *Buck Rogers*!" Ozzie screams. Then I hear him going up to the third floor where Papa is. I hear him say, "Please, Papa, please come down. You never miss *Buck Rogers*."

This is sad. But Papa doesn't come.

We go on down and start listening. *Buck Rogers* always begins the same way. There is a thundering, rumbling sound. That is supposed to be the time machine that takes us into the future and forward in time to go with Buck. And if The Frink is here, as he usually is waiting for Gwen, he always says, "You know how they really make those sound effects? They bang on a piece of sheet metal and then they . . ." And every week we tell him to shut up, or, if

Mama's around, to be quiet. It just ruins it. It is supposed to be the time machine, not sheet metal getting banged on. Then after the roar the announcer says, "Buck Rogers . . . in the . . . twenty-fifth cen-tu-reeee." And then there is the commercial for Cocomalt that you stir in your milk—we hate it. Number six on the vomitron. Then the show really begins. Here's how it began tonight:

"Wilma." (That's his assistant. She's gorgeous. We just know that even though we can't see her.) "Wilma, does all your equipment check out?" Buck asks.

"Yes, Buck, I have my thermic radiation Projector, the electro-cosmic spectrometer and the super-radiating protonoformer all set to go."

Ozzie just loves it when they have the super-radiating protonoformer. But it probably won't seem the same tonight without Papa being here. I really do feel sorry for Ozzie.

JUST BEFORE BED

Guess what? Papa came down in the middle of the program. Now the frost on the window was about to melt from Ozzie beaming, although Mama was

48

about as happy. Then after the show Papa dug into his pocket and came up with some bits of copper wiring and a couple of capacitors that Luther, the foreman at Greenhandle's, said he didn't need. It probably amounted to all of three cents but it really takes very little to make Ozzie happy. Just Papa to listen to *Buck Rogers* with him and a few metal bits.

Toward the end of the show, Buck always says something kind of philosophical and really nice to Wilma like, "And don't forget, Wilma, you are an important part of this mission for the peace and security of the planets." I kept thinking about that when we got into bed. It was snowing out but kind of slow snow, if you know what I mean. The flakes just sort of drifted down and we could see the moon. Twenty-three more days until Christmas and I don't have to worry about the peace and security of the planet, but I do worry about Papa. I wonder if this stupid Depression will be over by the twenty-fifth century, certainly not the twenty-fifth of December. Everyone is really counting on Franklin Roosevelt. I hope he doesn't let us down. He's not exactly Buck Rogers, and Mrs. Roosevelt is no Wilma Deering, but the Roosevelts are real and Buck and Wilma aren't.

P.S. I'm a little bit hungry tonight. We had cabbage au gratin and a casserole of Spanish rice with a little bit of pork. Lady called this dish rumor of pork. But the au gratin didn't seem to stretch as far as it usually does. And you practically need a microscope to see the pork in the Spanish rice. I didn't realize I was hungry until *Buck Rogers* stopped. Nothing like a good story to take your mind off your stomach. I don't think you feel quite as empty when you're listening to a good radio show or reading a good book.

DECEMBER 3, 1932

The worst thing has happened. I can't really even write about it. We are all just shocked. Mr. Otis, Bernadette's father, killed himself! Yes, it really happened and just as we were arriving for the birthday party. We hadn't even taken off our coats. We heard this awful sharp crack. Nothing like the sound effects on the radio. Then a scream and then Bernadette's grandmother came rushing down the stairs and hustled us all out the door and told us to go home. So we did. Now we just found out. I can't write another word.

5 P.M.

Willie Faye is a mess. She kind of froze up after we found out and she won't speak. Mama's real worried. She made her Ovaltine and ran a hot bath for her, but Willie Faye just sits on the bed holding Tumbleweed. I don't know what to do.

6 P.M.

Willie Faye won't eat supper.

7 P.M.

Mama's a mess. She was sitting in the dark in the sunroom, of all places, the coldest part of the house in the evening. She was all bundled up and crying. I know what she's crying about. She's worried about Papa. He hardly ate any dinner, then went up to his room—k-chirp.

7:15 P.M.

Clem is a mess. She broke down and told me tonight that Olive Winslow's father has left their family. Just up and left. He had lost his job and the Hoosier Bank that closed had most of their savings in it. She hadn't wanted to say anything but when she heard the news about Mr. Otis she just had to tell somebody. Gwen is out in the sunroom in the dark talking to Mama. They don't even have a light on. It's just all shadowy. On the wall of the sunroom Mama had a painting student from the John Herron Art School come and make a mural of Greek goddesses holding baskets of fruit. But you can't see the goddesses or the fruit now. Just two hunched figures in the dark.

7:30 P.M.

Lady is not a mess. She is putting on her lipstick and powdering her nose and asked me to look in that tangle of an underwear drawer of hers for a garter. Nothing stops Lady from going out. "Where are you going?" I ask nastily. Lady suddenly tucks her lips in and looks a bit shamefaced. But then she perks right up. Lady cannot endure sadness or anything like it for more than a second or two.

"Where are we going?" she says.

"We?" I ask.

"Yes, you, me, and Willie Faye and Ozzie are going to the movies."

"What are we going to see?"

"*Red Dust* with Clark Gable and Jean Harlow."

I am just thankful that it is not *Anna Christie* with Greta Garbo. Lady has seen that movie eight times! I don't think Ozzie will ever agree to see this *Red Dust* thing. Ozzie hates kissy-face movies, as he calls them. His tastes are strictly horror.

Ozzie agrees to go, and so does Willie Faye.

DECEMBER 4, 1932

Just after supper—and how could I have eaten knowing this!

Willie Faye has seen a dead body! I've never known any kid who has seen an actual dead body, and the one Willie Faye saw was her own mother's! So now I know why she froze up when Mr. Otis shot himself. Willie Faye not only saw her mother's dead body but LIVED with it for two whole days before

53

the neighbors came and got the coroner. Is that not the limit? I wanted to ask her all sorts of questions like, Did her mother's body start to change color or begin to smell? Did she touch it? But I knew that would be, as Gwen says, "extremely insensitive." I was very glad that Ozzie wasn't around because he would have asked.

Willie Faye said that finally after two days, the neighbors came by, the ones who went to California in the jalopy, and that they went back and got the coroner from Heart's Bend, which was more than fifteen miles away. The coroner came in his special car for picking up dead bodies. Willie Faye said she would have buried the body herself but she couldn't lift it, and she was afraid that she wouldn't have the strength to dig deep enough and that the coyotes would get it, or that the dust storms would just blow it right out of the grave.

Mama just poked her head in and said we should be doing our homework!

AFTER SORT OF DOING OUR HOMEWORK

I can't imagine living where Willie Faye did out there in Heart's Bend, Texas. She told me some more about it. The town itself has only nine buildings: a jail, a saloon, a feed store, a dry goods store, the coroner's house, the sheriff's house, and three others that were empty. Oh, yes, there had been a train depot but then the train stopped going there. She said nobody ever wanted to get off in Heart's Bend, and nobody from Heart's Bend ever went anyplace.

She told me the story about the first time the train, the Lone Star, just went on through and never stopped. It was kind of sad because before that she would always try to go down to the depot to watch the Lone Star on Saturdays when her parents went to town. She said she loved watching it pull into the depot. The train was silver and sleek. It reminded her of a shooting star, it was so fast looking. The conductor would get off the train. She said he was the only man in Texas who didn't wear overalls or denim britches and a cowboy hat. No, he wore a black suit with a vest under the jacket and he had a gleaming gold chain that stretched across the vest with a big watch on it. On his head he wore a boxy little hat with a patent leather bill and there was gold braid on the hat.

Willie Faye showed me a picture she had drawn of the conductor and the train. It was really good. Anyhow, one Saturday she was down there and the Lone Star just shot right through. Willie Faye said it didn't even slow down. It just raced on, and the noise of its roar became dimmer and dimmer and finally vanished. She felt that it was as if Heart's Bend didn't even exist anymore. And she never saw the conductor again.

Mama has come back in to check on us. She heard us talking. We have to go back to pretending to be doing homework. That's why I am writing all this down now. It looks like I am doing homework. But I want to hear more about Heart's Bend. Will do three math problems, then ask Willie Faye to tell me more.

THREE MATH PROBLEMS LATER

(I did them all wrong. I don't even care. Willie Faye's story is more interesting than common denominators.)

• • •

When Willie Faye started talking again she told me the most curious thing. She said that about a month after the last time the train stopped in Heart's Bend, a terrible dust storm came through and scoured off the *B* from the signpost for the town. She said it seemed kind of like the town had just given up on itself because now the sign read Heart's end.

We were really quiet for a while after she told me that. I didn't know what to say. Then she began telling me a few other things. And I started to realize how really little we knew about Willie Faye. It was just like she and Tumbleweed blew in here a week ago and we never really found out about her. I mean it's like she just got caught up in our own Swift family whirly wind. She said that she has never in her life been in a place like our house or met people like us. She said we were "a wonder." She said she can't imagine Martians, even if they are green, being any stranger than Lady.

Willie Faye said she never knew people could have so many "gol-darned opinions about things." She said that the other evening when we were talk-ing about Kate Smith's hairdo not looking good on

Mama that we talked for more than ten minutes. And that after the movie we talked at least another ten about Clark Gable's dimples and Jean Harlow's hair. So I asked her if she was bored with all this talk. And she sat bolt upright in bed. "Bored!" she said. "You must be plumb nuts. You're just as good as the movies." And she had never seen a movie, either, before yesterday.

I think it was very quiet in Willie Faye's family. She was the only child. And it was very empty out there in Texas. She said there was nothing but sky and scrubland that used to be good for raising cotton and cattle but not anymore. Her father had died the year before her mother but she hadn't seen his body. They had a little bit of land on which they raised cotton and had a few cows and chickens and pigs. I guess that's why she's good with our chickens. She said if Jackie were sick or something she could kill the chickens for us. It was easy and didn't take much strength. She said what took strength was chopping cotton and butchering cattle. They had mostly milk cows but their cows had almost given up on making milk because it hadn't rained in so long and cows need green grass for milk. She said there weren't even any trees out there.

Then she asked me something odd. She asked about the jars on the top pantry shelf. She said, "Are those peaches?" And I told her yes. And she said something that struck me so peculiar. She said, "I've heard of peaches." Now, can you imagine that—"hearing" about peaches? It struck me as so queer—hearing about peaches. So then I asked her if she would like to try eating one instead of just hearing about it. And she thought a little bit and said, "Oh, you don't have to go to that trouble."

I told her it was no trouble. But she seemed kind of shy about trying it. So I said, "Well, how would you like to go downstairs and just look at them, then make up your mind?" So right now we're going to wait a few more minutes until we're sure everyone is asleep. Then we'll go downstairs and look at the peaches. Lady just stirred in her bed but she can sleep through anything.

DECEMBER 5, 1932—DAWN!

Willie Faye and I have stayed up all night! I have never done that in all my life. It's sort of wonderful. You feel as if you have slipped in an extra day of life while the rest of the world was asleep. After we got downstairs in the pantry to look at the peaches we just weren't tired, so we thought, Why go back to bed? Let's just stay up. It's been really fun, but first I have to tell you about the peaches and what we did. We got down there in the pantry and outside it had snowed, a lot more than we ever thought. The moon reflecting off all that snow lit up the pantry with a real nice wintry glow, and those peaches that Mama put up last summer just gleamed like dozens of little suns in their glass jars. I convinced Willie Faye that she should try one. So I climbed up on the counter and got a jar. Then I got this crazy idea. It was so beautiful outside. The night was all polka-dotty with falling snow. So I said, "How about we put our coats over our pajamas and get some galoshes out of the closet and eat our peaches on the back steps?" Sometimes it's fun to do something just plain nutty. Willie Faye thought that was a terrific idea. So we did.

I can't describe how lovely it was out there in all this snowy silence. The neighborhood so very quiet and just the click of our spoons on our dishes and the peaches in their thick sweet syrup tasting better than ever. I told Willie Faye how every summer we would go to Brown County, south of Indianapolis, where friends of Mama and Papa's have a farm. They let us pick the peaches in their orchard and we picnic. There is a pond nearby for swimming. Yes, I told her all this on the snowy back steps. And the snow was so clean and white that after we finished our peaches we scooped some snow up with our spoons and stirred it in with the leftover syrup in our bowls. It was the best!

This has been a very strange weekend. I mean, it starts off with Mr. Otis blasting his head off with a shotgun and then Willie Faye gets to see her first movie and eat her first peach. And then I learn about her peculiar little town that lost the *B* out of its name and her poor dead mother. It seems as if Willie Faye and I have done a lifetime of living just in the last two days. Well, it's back to school in three hours!

AFTER SCHOOL

I've graduated from being a sheep to a shepherd in the Christmas pageant. I'm supposed to be pleased. Ho! Ho! Ho! as Santa would say. Willie

Faye, however, has a great part. She's an angel. The littlest angel. They're going to have to cut down the wings for her. She is so excited. Here is another thing that Willie Faye has never done: worn a costume! I said, "Didn't you ever go trick-or-treating at Halloween?" Then I remembered that she lived fifteen miles out of town and that the nearest neighbors were eight miles away. So I guess Heart's Bend would not be the best trick-or-treating territory.

Lucy Meyers and Betty Hodges are shepherds, too, so that makes it more fun. We all walked partway home from school together. We passed the Otis's house and saw cars lined up and people paying calls. The funeral is tomorrow. Bernadette won't be back in school until after Christmas. Martine Vontill informed us of this in her usual stuck-up, snotty way and told us that she is in charge of getting Bernadette's homework to her and helping her keep up.

We took a real ziggy-zaggy way home so we could see what folks are putting up for Christmas decorations. The Tarkingtons always do it up grand, and sure enough, we saw two colored men outside stringing up lights and Mr. Booth Tarkington himself directing them in his galoshes and overcoat. I decided to stop and say hello. I had met him once and I thought, Wouldn't this be just the tops if Willie Faye could meet him. So I called out, "Mr. Tarkington, it's me, Minerva Swift, Sam and Belle's daughter. Your house sure is going to look pretty."

Well, would you believe it, the greatest living author in America came right down across his lawn to say hello. I introduced Willie Faye. I told him her whole story—well, of course not her whole story, not about her mother's dead body. But I did tell him about how she came here with her cat from Heart's Bend and how she had never seen a city like Indianapolis before because Heart's Bend had only nine buildings and was missing the *B* on its sign. He seemed genuinely taken by Willie Faye and then he said something kind of curious. He said, "You might be a writer someday, Miss Minerva." And I said, "Why's that, Mr. Tarkington?" And he said, "Only a writer would comment on a town missing a letter on its signpost, and what a letter to miss in this case!" Well, that just about made my day. But of course it means that Willie Faye could be a writer, too, because after all, she is the one who first told me about it.

. . .

When we got home Ozzie was in an uproar about two things—one good, one bad. The good thing is that the famous German scientist Albert Einstein is going to be allowed to live in America. It was in the newspaper. Clem of course is an expert on all this. She says it's because of this new fellow in Germany, Adolf Hitler, and his National Socialist German Workers' party, which is gaining strength all the time in elections. They are against Jewish people. Ozzie says that Albert Einstein is the smartest man on earth. Then he's off and running. "He invented the theory of special relativity and then he figured out that light exists and travels in little packets. . . ." I don't really understand any of this but I'm used to Ozzie blathering on about particles and motion. However, I now see all this from Willie Faye's point of view. Ozzie is talking a mile a minute about things that she had never even thought about, like the speed of light. So that's the good thing that has Ozzie in an uproar. The bad thing is that while we were watching *Red Dust*, "that stupid old kissy-face movie," Ozzie found out that *Freaks* was playing at another theater. In this movie a woman is transformed into a half-human, half-chicken creature, and then there is another creature called The Living Torso. Ozzie is determined to see it this weekend.

DECEMBER 6, 1932

Holy smokes. Lady is in big trouble. She was over at Letty Cohen's last night and she bleached her hair to look like Jean Harlow. Mama is furious and says Tudor Hall will kick her out. She looks pretty funny going off to school this morning in her uniform. Somehow platinum blond hair doesn't go with a blue serge uniform and oxford shoes.

AFTER SCHOOL

Lady is even in bigger trouble — more than just the blond hair. First of all she got a D+ on her Latin test. Why do they even bother with a plus when it's a D? Anyway, when Miss Crowe handed her the test, Lady said, supposedly under her breath, "Just gimme a viskey, ginger ale on the side, and don't be stingy, baby." That's what Greta Garbo says in the movie *Anna Christie*. Lady has such a sassy mouth and she can't resist being the class clown. She said everybody just fell to pieces laughing, except for Miss Crowe. Mama has to go in for a talk with the headmistress.

Papa said that if Willie Faye and I finish our homework he will take us downtown to look at the Ayres department store Christmas angel and all the store decorations. But he said that Lady can't go and that she has to stay home and take that "infernal color" out of her hair and put back in her regular color. I haven't heard Papa so angry since the time I said that the hot dog au gratin made me sick to even look at.

LATER

We had so much fun downtown. We took the trolley and it seemed as if everyone on it was going down to see the decorations. There were a lot of jokes about how it doesn't cost anything to look. I guess everyone was feeling like us that there would not be much we could afford to buy. Papa seemed more like his old self. All the stores were bright and gay. And I think the Christmas angel on top of the Ayre's clock looks exactly like Willie

Faye. Even Papa thought so. We saw the prettiest things in the store. Papa saw a dress I know he would have loved to buy for Mama. It was in the window at Strauss's. He said, "Now, doesn't that dress have a lot of the go-to-the-dickens about it." "Go-to-the-dickens" is one of Papa's favorite expressions. I haven't heard him say it in a long time.

I saw a snappy plaid tie that I would have loved to buy for Papa. But it was two dollars! And the dress that Papa liked was twelve!! "I wish you could buy that for Mama," I said.

"I wish I could, too, sweetheart, but you know what your mama would say. She'd say, 'Sam, there are better ways to spend that money than hanging a pretty dress on me.'"

The best part of the trip was the Chocolate Girls. Yes, there were these pretty young ladies dressed up in dainty white ruffled caps and aprons, and they were passing out a new chocolate treat, *for free*, that is being made by the Walter Baker Chocolate Company. We each had two. They were scrumptious.

The only not so good parts of the trip were when we passed the Hoosier Bank and Trust. All closed up. Papa shook his head. I think Greenhandle's did a lot of banking business through the Hoosier Bank and Trust and Papa knows a lot of the bank officers. So he was probably thinking about them being out of work. Mr. Mertz was the bank president and a very important man in Indianapolis. Mama always said his suits were beautifully tailored. And he always wore a handsome watch chain across his vest. Now, what happens to a really important man with fine suits and a gold watch chain when he can't go to work anymore? He might not even want to get out of his pajamas in the morning. I started thinking about this, and well, it made me very sad.

The other thing that made me sad was when we went by that corner of New York and Meridian. I couldn't help but think of Mr. Otis selling apples. But I don't think Papa thought of him.

I just don't know what I am going to do for Christmas presents. Mama always says it's the thought that counts. But it really is hard to have thoughts with no money.

DECEMBER 7, 1932

Ozzie tried to help Lady with her hair while we were downtown last night. The problem was that in order for Lady's dark hair to turn blond all her natural color had to be stripped out. So Lady couldn't exactly do what Papa asked. There was no regular color left to put back in. But Ozzie went into his lab — a fatal trip, if you ask me. You should see what Lady looks like this morning. Clem calls the color orangutan red. Mama is beside herself. Jackie screamed when Lady came downstairs. They say that chickens aren't smart, but it was Lady's turn to feed them this morning and one of them just stared at her kind of dumbfounded. Can you beat that!

AFTER SCHOOL

It started raining while we were in school today and all the pretty snow has turned icky. I hate it when it does this right before Christmas. It's too warm but not sunny. Everything is just drab and gray. Everything except Lady's hair.

LATER

Yikes! Lady's chopped off her hair. She looks like Little Orphan Annie gone berserk. She said she had to because Mama was going to take her to the hairdresser and it would have cost almost two dollars to dye it back. So she just decided to cut it. Lady really does feel bad. This is a first. I don't think Lady has ever felt guilty or bad about anything she's done. She says she'll wear a scarf until it grows out.

We're rushing to get our homework done so we can listen to *The Shadow*. Actually there isn't much work to do because we spend an awful lot of time rehearsing for this stupid Christmas pageant. Being a shepherd isn't bad because we just pretend to sleep in this heap off to stage left. We don't have to do anything until they get to that part in Luke about the shepherds. "And there were in the same country shepherds abiding in the field, keeping watch over their flock by night and the shepherds said to one another, 'Lo! Let us go now to Bethlehem, and see this thing which the Lord hath made known to us,'" etc., etc. "Lo" is our cue. So we relax until we get to "Lo."

Well, Betty brought this magazine that has all of

these movie star pictures in it. I have found someone more handsome than Clark Gable: Gary Cooper. I swoon for Gary Cooper. Luckily I was lying down already. I wonder what Gary Cooper would think of me. Golly, all done up in this stupid shepherd outfit and carrying a crook at that. I wish I had bosoms. I'm as flat as a pancake. Guess it doesn't matter if I'm wearing this shepherd stuff. Yards and yards of stinky old cheesecloth in the ugliest colors — maroon and orange. I really doubt if the shepherds in Bethlehem in those days wore these colors.

AFTER DINNER

Another stupid aspic for dinner. It's a Christmas one — red and green. A ten on the vomitron. But I ate it and did not complain because Mama and Papa were so quiet. Between Lady's hair, the Hoosier Bank and Trust closing, and the rumors of the Hocklemeyer Auto Company closing, things aren't exactly joyous. No one can believe it about Hocklemeyer's. That will be terrible for Greenhandle's. Papa barely said a word tonight. Hocklemeyer's is the oldest auto manufacturing company in Indianapolis. They used to make carriages. A Hocklemeyer auto has been in every single one of the famous Indianapolis 500-mile races since the races started.

Papa didn't even come down to listen to *The Shadow* tonight. But Willie Faye, Ozzie, Lady, and I were all sitting there as soon as John Barclay, the most boring man in the world, came on to talk about Blue Coal. That's the sponsor and John Barclay is the president of the Blue Coal Fuel Company. It's the most boring advertisement about how to reduce heating costs. And he has a very annoying voice. But then the real announcer comes on for the show and there is this weird laugh and this really spooky voice says, "The weed of crime bears bitter fruit." Then creepy music and the voice speaks once more. "Who knows what evil lurks in the heart of man. . . . The Shadow knows!"

The Shadow is Lamont Cranston and he's invisible. Ozzie and I are nuts for Lamont Cranston. Actually he's not exactly invisible. He went to the Orient where he learned "the power to cloud men's minds." He sort of hypnotizes people so they can't see him. Then he goes about solving crimes. Tonight's episode was called "The

Unburied Dead." Really, really creepy! Usually when we listen Lady is bad-mouthing Margo Lane, The Shadow's sidekick. Lady thinks he is very "patronizing," as she puts it, to Margo. She says it's like he is always looking down at her and she never gets to really be in on the action. She's just there to say, "Oh, Lamont, be careful." Or "Lamont, you shouldn't go in there by yourself." But tonight Lady was very quiet.

After we went to bed, Mama came in and said that tomorrow she is going over to the Otises to deliver a hot dish and that she expects me to go with her, but Willie Faye doesn't have to come. The last thing I want to do: deliver a hot dish to a family in mourning.

DECEMBER 8, 1932

Betty and Lucy and I got kicked out of the Christmas pageant rehearsal today and sent to the principal's office. I pray that Miss Gordon won't call Mama. Mama might just have a heart attack. First Lady, now me. And Hocklemeyer's *is* shutting down. This could push Mama over the brink. Here's what happened in rehearsal. We were doing our usual thing "sleeping" but talking. Now, our cue, as I have said, is the word "Lo!" Unfortunately when the narrator got to the "Lo" part in the Gospel According to Luke we were giggling madly, not thinking about "Lo" at all. I had started to think about my bosoms again. Not just mine and having them or not. I started to think what a funny-sounding word "bosoms" is. So I started to snicker and snort just a little. Then Lucy asked what I was laughing about so I told her. Then before you know it she and Betty and I were just having convulsions. I mean, "bosoms" is really a funny word if you think about it. It was just awful in Miss Gordon's office when she asked what we had been laughing about. Well, we practically fell down on the floor laughing again. We all had to stay after school, and when I got home Mama was furious because we would be late going over to the Otises and delivering the hot dish. I didn't tell Mama why I was late. I just said I had forgotten about the Otises.

LATER

It was torturous! Even walking there was torturous because the hot dish was tuna and I hate tuna hot dish. It stinks. I had the geography assignment from Miss Cuddy — some mimeographed maps and lists of natural resources — to give to Bernadette. So we had to walk three blocks down Meridian and then three over to Central with me smelling tuna hot dish. Definitely number ten on the vomitron. By the time we got there I was almost ready to throw up, and if I needed a little nudge Martine Vontill was there to provide it. She actually opened the door. "I already brought Bernadette the geography maps for the anthracite coal deposits in western Pennsylvania." Those were her first words! Can you believe it? Well, what was left for me to say but, "I brought tuna hot dish." Then she said, "Oh, I'll take that." And rushed off to the kitchen. Even Mama looked a little startled. It was as if Martine and her mother had taken over the whole household.

We were shown into the living room. Mrs. Otis was sitting on a couch. She held a hanky, or rather, had it twisted around her hand. Grief has done Mrs. Otis no favors. I always thought that Mrs.

Otis's face looked, well, kind of furnished. That is the only word I can think of—"furnished" with overstuffed sofas. Yes, her nose actually reminds me of a love seat. It swoops down in the middle and plumps out at each nostril into two cushiony nubs that are now very red. For that matter, her whole body seems upholstered, puffy and overstuffed. But her eyes were dim behind a mist of grief.

Bernadette sat beside her on the couch. Bernadette's face is just the opposite of her mother's. Her features seem stranded on her face, too small for the space they occupy. They are like little teensy islands in the middle of a vast ocean. Her nose was like a little pink dot and she sniffled some. I didn't know what to say, so I muttered something about anthracite deposits and the coal map of western Pennsylvania. I know—stupid! I couldn't figure out anything else to say.

Luckily another lady came in with a chafing dish full of something. Somehow she had slipped by Martine. So Bernadette got up to take the dish into the kitchen. I just sat there and said nothing. Mama talked in a very quiet voice to Mrs. Otis. She seemed to know the right things to say. I just sort of looked around. The Otis's house is pretty dismal and it's not just because of Mr. Otis blasting his head off. Frankly it's just downright ugly. They have these little crocheted doilies over everything — the arms of chairs, tables. Once upon a time I suppose they were white, but now they are yellow. On a sideboard they have one of the ugliest decorations I have ever seen. It is a glass dome that stands more than a foot high with waxed fruit all piled up under it. I was so glad when Mama said it was time to go, I nearly smiled. I remembered not to in the nick of time. But then something else happened. I don't know why I thought of it right at that moment. Darned if I didn't think of bosoms! I felt a huge burble of laughter start to well up in me and just then Martine came back in with Bernadette. This might have been the most physically painful moment of my entire life. If I burst out laughing now . . . Well, I just couldn't even think about it. I had to think of something else and not bosoms. I bit the insides of my mouth to keep from laughing. I was trying to think of the most dreadful, sad thoughts. Finally we got out of there! As I said, the whole visit was torture — start to finish. But at least when I got home there was *Charlie Chan* to look forward to. The O's, Olive and Opal, came over to listen with Clem. But Papa didn't come down this evening.

DECEMBER 9, 1932

Did much better on the spelling test today. But this time Willie Faye missed two words. I'm so happy it's Friday. One more week of school, then Christmas break. The O's — Olive and Opal — came over again. We all listened to *Buck Rogers*. But Papa didn't come down at all! This is just getting creepy. Sometimes I feel that Papa is just kind of fading away from us, getting dimmer and dimmer. He hardly ever talks. I can't imagine what he is doing up there in that room all the time. What if one morning he gets up and just never comes downstairs? I keep thinking, What is he not telling us? Maybe we don't have enough money for food for the rest of the week. I try not to eat too much at supper. It was rumor of pork again. It's hard, though. We all like doing the dishes now because we stand behind the icebox door and lick the casserole pots before we put them in the sink to wash. Mama would kill us if she saw us doing that.

Anyhow, Papa didn't come down and he missed Jack Benny. He shouldn't have. Jack Benny is REALLY funny. I think it would have made Papa feel a teensy bit better to hear his jokes. The O's say that Groucho Marx now has a radio show and that he's even funnier. After we listened to Jack Benny we all went upstairs to Clem and Gwen's room. Gwen is out with The Frink and Lady is out with her gang. Wouldn't you know that Lady has sewn up a mess of gorgeous scarves to cover her hair—ones with fringes and beads and little crystals. She has even made herself a turban. It is a satin turban and she plans to wear it to the Christmas Tinsel Time Dance at the Athletic Club. Meanwhile I was thinking how positively frumpy we all look—about as fashionable as a dog's breakfast. Just as I'm thinking how unfashionable we are, who comes whooping up the stairs but Lady. "I'm here for a costume change!" she announces gaily. Then she stops and looks at Clem and the O's. She shakes her head and says, "Girls, it's Friday night. You're coming with me."

"Where?" I sit up on the bed. This sounds so exciting. "Not you, Minnie. You're too young." Too young! I am furious. "Come on, Clem, come on, O's, we're going out!" she yells. And this is truly unbelievable: Lady works magic on those three girls who thirty minutes before looked like dogs' breakfasts. She shows them how to put on makeup, and she fixes their hair and ties what she calls a bandeau around Olive's head, then teases out some little curls from underneath it. Then she goes into Papa and Mama's room. Papa's upstairs k-chirping, of course, and she says he won't miss these for one night. Well, I can't believe it but she has a pair of his tuxedo pants. She puts Clem in those and hikes them up with the satin cummerbund so she won't stumble over them. She finds a close-fitting black sweater for her to wear on top and then throws a satin shawl she made for a prom over the whole thing. Clem looks sensational. Clem can't even believe it herself. She blinks at her reflection in the mirror. "It's very Greta Garbo," Lady says.

"How did you ever think this up, Lady?" Clem asks.

Lady has a good answer. "It's amazing what wearing a uniform five days a week and going to an all-girls' school does for one's imagination."

For Opal she got one of Gwen's old tea dresses

and then — this is the most outrageous — she ran downstairs and got a summer-weight tablecloth from the camphor chest. She draped it over the dress and around Opal's hips and somehow knotted it into a rosette right below her waist. It looked exactly like a dress that the new Hollywood movie star Wynne Gibson was wearing in a picture in the newspaper the other day. It wasn't a tea dress anymore, it was "bewitching" — that's what the newspaper said about Wynne Gibson's dress.

Willie Faye just sat there on the bed the whole time with her mouth hanging open. She had never seen anything like it. This was probably the most entertainment she had ever experienced in her life. But it wasn't enough for me. I felt completely left out. I knew where those girls were going. They were going to sneak down to the Tick Tock Club or the Cotton Club or the Paradise, down to Indiana Avenue where the jazz clubs are and all the great colored people play. I had heard Lady talk about it. Mama and Papa would up and die if they knew that Lady did this. But I'm no tattletale. Still I felt rotten. And of course they would just tell Mama a fib. They would say they were going to the Indiana Theater, which is a very proper place to go hear music. Or that there was a band playing at the Circle Theater. Most of the musicians who come there are white — big bands. It isn't really jazz. Lady likes jazz. Her favorite musician is one named Scrapper. He plays both the piano and the guitar. Lady says you hadn't heard anything until you've heard Scrapper Blackwell play Funky Boogie.

DECEMBER 10, 1932

Dawn! It is dawn and Lady and Clem and the O's just got back in! And you know, I don't think Mama even noticed. Sometimes I think Mama is just too tired and too worried about Papa and Greenhandle's to worry about us. I woke up when I heard them creeping into the room. They all looked giddy and their eyes were shining. I couldn't believe it — Clem and the O's out on the town, looking not just snappy but glamorous. Those three were the biggest Goody Two-Shoes ever — well, Goody Six-Shoes.

But I'm going back to sleep. It's Saturday.

LATER

Willie Faye woke me up—earlier than I wanted. Lady is still asleep and I bet she will be until noon. The O's and Clem are still asleep as well in Clem and Gwen's room. What a night they all had. Willie Faye says we have to get cracking with Christmas presents. We have to think up something, she said. I had no idea of what we should do. This is a Christmas that needs magic. If I had my druthers I would magically reopen Hocklemeyer's auto manufacturing plant and that would make Papa happy. And Mama, too, for that matter. I'd get Lady's hair to grow back magically. For Clem I would find her a genuinely handsome beau. For Gwen I would get a magic carpet and fly her to Paris, France, where she could write about more interesting things than aspic, eat better food than aspic, and fall in love with a Frenchman instead of Delbert Frink, who to my mind is the boyfriend version of aspic—with salad oil on top. I guess when you don't have any money for Christmas presents the only way to think is magically. Willie Faye says that's just silly. We don't need magic. She said look what she's done with chicken feathers. And it is true. She has made these pretty earrings for Lady with the chicken feathers.

Well, then something magical did happen. It was the strangest coincidence. We just got downstairs for breakfast and I looked out the window and saw Jackie coming up the drive with two big fat fluffy things under her arms. "What in the world?" Mama said.

Then Jackie poked her head in the kitchen door and we heard cluckings. "I done got you a Rhode Island Red and a guinea hen. They'se the best-laying chickens in the world."

But Willie Faye and I just looked at each other, our eyes nearly popping out. These chickens also had the most beautiful feathers we'd ever seen. The guinea hen had these glossy black feathers with little white speckles and the Rhode Island Red wasn't just red. She was russet and orange and scarlet. Why, she was brighter than a maple tree in October. Willie Faye dragged me out of the breakfast room. "But what will we make?" I asked.

"Hats!"

"But I don't know how to make a hat."

"Lady will," Willie Faye said.

She was probably right but I had another

question. "How will we get the feathers?"

"Leave that to me," Willie Faye said.

I remembered how she told me she could kill a chicken. So I blurted out, "You can't kill them, Willie Faye!"

"'Course not. Don't worry. I'll take care of the feathers. You and Lady figure out the hat-making part."

Then Gwen, who had been reading the paper, gave a little yelp. "Mama!" she shrieked. Willie Faye and I raced into the kitchen. "Mama," she said, "you and Papa shouldn't have."

"What shouldn't they have done?" I asked.

Gwen looked at me. "Mama and Papa gave twelve dollars to the Santa Fund."

Twelve dollars! That was the exact amount of the pretty dress that we saw downtown with Papa. And Papa had said that Mama wouldn't stand for it. That she'd say, "Sam, there are better ways to spend that money than hanging a pretty dress on me."

Willie Faye, Clem, the O's, and I are going to the movies tonight when Mama and Papa go to the Dramatic Club Christmas party. Not *Freaks*. *Freaks* was banned in Indianapolis. It's been banned in

Detroit and St. Louis and someplace else. Ozzie is furious. He's going to stay home and work on his homemade telephone. He's crushing up charcoal because that's what you need, he says — compressible carbon for varying the conductivity in the electrical signal that can be amplified at the other end to make the sound. When Ozzie started explaining this, Willie Faye's eyes just got real wide. I could see that she was having a hard time deciding whether to go with us to the movies — a double bill of *Strange Interlude* with Norma Shearer and Clark Gable and *Grand Hotel* with Greta Garbo and John Barrymore — or stay home and crush charcoal with Ozzie.

TEN MINUTES LATER

I can't believe it. She's staying home! Well, as Mama says, "You can lead a horse to water but you can't make it drink."

DECEMBER 11, 1932

Oh, dear! When we came home from the movies last night, Mama was here. We couldn't believe it.

She was supposed to be going to the Dramatic Club party. When we left she had been getting dressed. Lady had restyled her old chocolate-brown velvet tea gown and made it into a real dancing dress. It was just gorgeous with these huge puffy shirred sleeves. But Mama and Papa never went to the dance. It was so sad. When we came in Mama was sitting out in the sunroom — always a bad sign — still wearing her gown and her fur scarf. We were all shocked. Willie Faye was really shocked when she came down from Ozzie's lab — not because Mama was still here but because she had never seen a fur scarf before. Fur scarves are kind of a shock if you've never seen one. They are made up from the skins of little foxes with the heads, tails, and paws still attached. Or I guess it can be minks or whatever you want. They even put little glass beads that look just like eyes in the foxes' heads. It's all just for decoration, not real warmth, but I guess if you've never seen one before it's a pretty weird decoration.

Anyhow, Mama said that Papa just didn't have the heart to go to the Dramatic Club party and then she sighed and said all he does is sit up in that little room tapping that adding machine.

"It's like he thinks there's magic in that machine and somehow money will fly out of it." So I guess I'm not the only one who's thinking that we need magic this Christmas. I didn't say anything, but I think it's the k-chirp of the typewriter I hear more than the k-chung of the adding machine. My ears are better than Mama's.

This is the dreariest day. I can't believe that Christmas is two weeks away. The weather has turned warm and drizzly and all the snow has gone. There's just slushy stuff left. Mud honey, Mama calls it.

The O's come over and we decide to bake Christmas cookies. Clem and the O's say we should take them to that shantytown over by the White River, Curtisville Bottom.

LATER

The house smells so good. So good that even Papa came down from his k-chirping or k-chunging to have a cookie. Mama looked so happy when she saw him. She went right over to him and gave him a hug. Usually I just hate it when they hug or kiss each other in front of us kids — they don't very often—but I was happy. It's gotten a lot colder outside. So even though there is no snow I'm getting more into the Christmas spirit. While Clem and the O's watched over the cookies, Willie Faye and I went up to discuss our chicken feather fashions with Lady. She thinks it's possible. She has a lot of felt that will be perfect for hats. Willie Faye was up early this morning and already has a bunch of feathers from the Rhode Island Red and the guinea hen. Guinea hens are REALLY stupid! Holy smokes, are they dumb. Willie Faye says that's good because they have the prettiest feathers.

Mama fixed a good dinner tonight. She opened a jar of green tomatoes that she had canned over the summer, and we had those fried up in batter and butter noodles and Welsh rarebit. I love Welsh rarebit. I love the way the cheese is melted over the bread. Ozzie and I drag our forks over the melting cheese and make designs—that is, until Mama catches us. Lady asked Mama when we might have meat again. I knew what she meant—real meat, like a roast, not rumor of pork. Mama just sighed. I saw a shadow pass over Papa's brow and I got all worried.

But then Willie Faye started telling this incredibly exciting story. I think it must have been the meat talk that reminded her. Willie Faye said that one night in Heart's Bend cattle rustlers came and slaughtered their only beef cow and butchered it right there in the field and hauled off all the meat. The only thing left from the animal was the head and the hooves. Then her father and the sheriff took off to chase them down. They got other people to help — a posse. That's what they call it when a sheriff leads a bunch of men to track down criminals out there. And they found a trail of blood — blood dripping from the butchered cattle, or so they thought. But it wasn't cattle. They found an actual dead person! A fellow named Sam Blount, and the rustlers had murdered him. He must have caught them trying to steal his cattle because his body was right beside the head of a butchered cow! Normally Mama wouldn't have let such talk take place at the table, but this was almost as good as a radio show — at least the way Willie Faye told the story. Mama did fan herself with her napkin even though it was cold inside and she said "Yee gads" about four times.

STILL LATER

You'll never guess what just happened. Clem was serenaded. I am NOT making this up! Clem has a beau! She met him when she went out with Lady and the O's Friday night and now here he is on Sunday, singing outside the window. Singing "My Darling Clementine"! This is the most exciting thing that ever happened to our family. I mean, of course it's not as exciting as what happened to Willie Faye's family's cow and the posse and all that. Ozzie says you can't beat a dead body lying next to the chopped-off head of a cow, but still this is pretty exciting. The beau's name is Marlon and he's from Minnesota and that is all Clem will tell us. She didn't invite him in but Mama said she could go out for a walk with him. It has gotten really, really cold. I wonder if she'll be warm enough. I wonder if she'll let him cuddle her. I couldn't see him that well but he kind of looked big and strong. I think as big as Clark Gable maybe.

DECEMBER 12, 1932

Too much excitement! When Willie Faye and I came down for breakfast this morning and we were sitting there eating our eggs, I happened to look out the window. I noticed the guinea hen sitting on a trash can. I looked about five or ten minutes later and I noticed that it was still there and hadn't moved a jot. So I got up and I said, "What's wrong with that hen?"

Then Jackie, who was just sliding some more eggs onto a plate for Papa, looked out and shrieked, "Lordy! Lordy! That darn stupid hen done gone and froze itself to the trash can."

Well, we all began screeching and yelling and throwing on our coats to rescue the guinea hen. We got outside and sure enough, it's frozen there. One of its feet was stuck solid. Mama sent me in for hot water. Then she yelled, "No, just bring my coffee cup. The kettle water will be too hot." So Jackie held the hen and Mama poured coffee on the hen's foot and pulled on it a little bit. We got the poor thing loose, but it seemed to be kind of in a state of shock. It collapsed in Jackie's arms with its beak hanging open, just as if it were swooning, like when Jean Harlow swooned in *Red Dust* except this was a chicken and Jackie is not Clark Gable.

So we got the creature inside and everyone fussed over it, and pretty soon Mama said, "Sam,

go to the basement and get the you-know-what."
Well, I didn't know what, but Papa seemed to
know what. He came back a few minutes later with
a bottle of clear fluid.

"What is that?" I asked.

"You hush up," Jackie said. Everyone seemed to
know except for me and Willie Faye. Finally Lady
dragged me off and told me it was gin! I couldn't
believe it. This is Prohibition. It's against the law
to sell or buy whiskey. I can't believe Mama and
Papa have a bottle of gin. But Lady said every
family has a bottle of something in their basement. So I asked why, because I never see Mama
or Papa drinking. Lady said they had it just "for
times like these." That I didn't understand at all.
Who can expect times like these? Who expects a
stupid guinea hen to freeze to their garbage can?
All this before eight o'clock in the morning! Must
rush to school. We're going to be late.

AFTER SCHOOL

The hen is still in the kitchen. Jackie fixed up a
basket for it. She put the basket in an old birdcage
we had because we were scared that Tumbleweed

might decide to eat the hen. She seems comfortable. Mama says that we can go with Clem and the O's to the shantytown and deliver cookies because Delbert Frink has offered to take Gwen there. As long as there is a young man she feels that we'll be safe. Delbert Frink couldn't protect us from an attacking guinea hen, to tell you the truth, but as long as we get to go, it's all right with me.

Oh, I nearly forgot to say that Jackie said she felt something was after that poor dumb guinea hen because its hind end was almost bald. Willie Faye and I looked at each other. The hat project is going nicely. We have all the felt cut out. We could use a few more feathers, however. Better switch to another chicken. That reminds me. The O's gave me an idea for other Christmas gifts: keepsake boxes made by lacquering pretty cutout pictures to wooden or cardboard boxes. I think I might make one for Willie Faye for Christmas. The only problem is that Willie Faye hardly has any keepsakes. I mean, the only things she brought with her were Tumbleweed and a few clothes, the pumpkin seeds, and that picture.

At school today they posted on the big bulletin board a picture that Willie Faye had drawn.

The assignment was to draw something in the classroom, anything. But Willie Faye was very imaginative. She drew the window, which looks out on the playground. She drew the window so exact—every little paint chip—and then through the window she showed a kind of blurry image of children playing. Miss Morse, the art teacher, said it was "very advanced." So even if you don't know about toilets, porcelain bathtubs, adjectives, Booth Tarkington, and *Charlie Chan* there is still stuff you can be advanced in.

DECEMBER 13, 1932

We went to the shantytown last night to deliver cookies. Delbert came, but guess who else came, too? Marlon! Marlon is so handsome and so nice and we could have all just killed Delbert. Delbert was so high and mighty and snooty to Marlon. Marlon is different. He comes from Minnesota and he's not a college graduate like Delbert but he's every bit as smart. You can just tell. He works as a lifeguard at the Antlers Hotel's indoor swimming pool and then he does half a dozen other things as well. He drives a truck and works in the shipping department at L. S. Ayres and Company, and he works part time at the jazz club where he and Clem met. But he has "lovely manners." Mama said that when he came by the house before we left for the shantytown with the cookies.

We all walked over to the shantytown. This is the one they call Curtisville. It is the biggest Hooverville in the state of Indiana even if they do call it after the vice president. It was a long, cold walk but I forgot the cold and my freezing feet when we got there. Honest to gosh, I saw people living in contraptions that you couldn't believe. I saw one family living in a pile of old tires covered with a tarp! Marlon said it was very dangerous. If all those tires collapsed they'd be squashed to death and there was a little baby, just a toddler. Then we saw ramshackle shacks with tin roofs made from flattened garbage cans. Garbage cans and oil drums were the most important part of Curtisville. People lit fires in them, cooked on them, flattened them into sheets for roofs or walls, and some people who were too tired to build anything just crawled into them and slept. I think they liked our cookies, but to tell you the truth, I felt a little stupid standing there with our cardboard boxes filled with cream cheese dainties, sugar cookies decorated like Santa Claus, and molasses crinkles. The children loved them, that's for sure. There was one little boy with the dirtiest face and I let him have a Santa Claus cookie, and he just stared and stared at it and then he turned his face up and he said, "Ma'am, if I don't eat this cookie, do you think it might through Christmas magic turn into a real Santa Claus?"

Well, I just didn't know what to say. But that Marlon was so nice. He just crouched down and said to the little boy, "I'm not sure, but would your mama and daddy like me to help them make your house safer?" Because it turned out that this indeed was the family that was living in the dangerous tire shack. Well, we had to go home but Marlon stayed there all night, I guess. He met Clem today after school and told her that he managed to get some wood and some metal cutters and had fixed them up something much safer. I don't know whether I'll ever get that little boy's face out of my mind. I don't think Mr. Roosevelt can become president quick enough. But we still have to wait until March. That's when his inauguration is. Who knows what could happen to that little boy by then? Who knows what could happen to *us* by then? But I know that we are better off than any of those people in Curtisville Bottom right now.

P.S. Papa never went to work today. But no one said anything. We just pretended that we didn't notice. I am not sure if that was the right thing to do or not.

DECEMBER 14, 1932

I don't know what I would do without the O's. They have been wonderful in helping me with the decoupage boxes. I am making one for Willie Faye and one for Ozzie. Ozzie's is going to be covered with comic strips and I am putting in it a spool of wire, six little capacitors, and some electrical tape. I'll go to Vonnegut's hardware store. I have two dollars saved up and I should be able to get all this stuff for Ozzie for less than a dollar.

Hardly any homework this week so plenty of time to work on Christmas presents. Willie Faye is really good at drawing dresses and fashions. She and Lady were talking about some skirt that Lady saw, and Willie Faye just picked up a pencil and sketched it out. So now Lady's got her sketching out all these fashion notions she has. Willie Faye seems to like doing it. She likes messing around in Ozzie's lab the most of all, though. She's helping him with his homemade telephone.

LATER

Marlon came over to visit Clem tonight. He listened to *The Shadow* with us and unlike Delbert did not try to explain all the sound effects and spoil the show for us. Then Delbert came. He asked Marlon in this really snooty way if he planned "ever to attend college and obtain a degree." Isn't that just the limit? I was practically dying when he said this. But it didn't faze Marlon at all. Marlon just said that if he ever had enough money, and the leisure time, he would like nothing better than to attend school — business school. "But in the meantime I try to learn from reading," he said.

"And what do you read, may I ask?" Delbert asked, so-o-o snottily.

"The *Wall Street Journal* and when I can get a

hold of it, the *London Financial Times*. I even read the quarterly reports of L. S. Ayres — you can learn a lot from those."

Delbert was dumbfounded. "You what?" he sputtered. "I thought you worked in shipping at Ayres."

"I do, and in trash removal. I found old copies of their quarterly reports from a year ago in a trash barrel. They were very instructive."

"And what did you learn?"

"I learned that the highest profit margin came from the nonessential but amusing items. In desperate times people want amusing things. That's why they go to the movies and listen to *The Shadow*. It doesn't have to be real but it does have to be amusing. They want a little magic."

Christmas magic! I thought. That's what we all want, and I remembered the little boy with the dirty face and his Santa Claus cookie. I wonder if he's eaten it yet.

DECEMBER 15, 1932

Bad news all the way around.

1) The *Indianapolis Star* reported that the Christmas angel from the big clock at Ayres was stolen! What horrible Scrooge would do that? Imagine stealing an angel. I hope it turns into a devil and punches the person in the nose. Ozzie thinks we should get a posse up and hunt it down. I told him they have posses only in the Wild West, not the Midwest.

2) The newspaper also reported that 19,437 people are officially out of work in Indianapolis. That is 9.5 percent of our workforce! And our Papa is one of them. Greenhandle's officially closed two days ago. Papa told us only this morning.

3) The guinea hen's frozen leg turned black and dropped off during the night. (This was not reported in the *Indianapolis Star.*)

So to sum up: Papa's out of work, we have a one-legged hen, and Indianapolis's official angel has been kidnapped. Merry Christmas!

Good news: We have only one more day of school. Of course we have to come back for the Christmas pageant performance on Sunday night, but that doesn't count. And tonight is *Charlie Chan*.

10 P.M. — AFTER *CHARLIE CHAN*

More good news: Gwen and Delbert Frink broke up! We are trying not to sound too happy but we are. I know it's because of the snooty way he treated Marlon. Gwen has a real sense of fair play and she would never hold it against anybody because they were not, as Lady says, "to the manor born." I think it means something to do with growing up with nice things and lots of money. But the truth is that Marlon has much better manners than Delbert, who was born with all that and went to Harvard to boot. I think Charlie Chan might have a proverb here. Actually what he said tonight would fit Delbert perfectly: "Slippery man sometimes slips in own oil."

DECEMBER 16, 1932

Last day of school!! No spelling test today, either. Just our class party. Willie Faye and I both made stained-glass-window cookies to bring for each of our class parties. You make gingerbread cookies and then cut out "windowpanes" inside the cookie. Then you poke holes in the top for ribbons to go through. Next you put crushed-up hard candies in different colors into the windowpanes and bake them on waxed paper. The hard candy bits melt and make pretty patches just like the stained glass windows in churches. They make the best ornaments to hang on Christmas trees. We are getting our Christmas tree today after school. We are going out to a place north of the city, a woods where you can saw down your own tree. Then we are coming back and going to have a tree-decorating party.

AFTER SCHOOL

Snow is expected so we are rushing to leave early to get our tree before the roads get bad. Jackie says we're going to have to kill the stupid hen. She is just too fat to walk on one leg and keeps falling over. Jackie says if you stew them up right they taste pretty good. So Mama nodded and said it was all right, and before you know it Jackie was out there in the garage wringing that hen's neck.

Willie Faye and I definitely have enough feathers now to finish our projects!

LATE, VERY LATE!

Mama said Willie Faye and I could stay up as late as we want. So now it's after midnight and Willie Faye is in Clem's room working on presents. I'm sick of stitching feathers on hats, so I thought I would write about what has been the best day in a long time. It's snowing now really hard. It started when we were out in Carmel — that's this little, teensy town, not even a town really, north of the city. It's really out in the country, not even in our county, but over in Hamilton County. There's mostly trees and woods. And now I found out something really special about Carmel. Back in the olden days when the town was first started, it was called Bethlehem! We learned that in our Indiana history class. So it is kind of fitting that we went there to get a Christmas tree, although as Lady points out, in the real Bethlehem they didn't exactly put up a Christmas tree and decorate it the night Jesus was born.

Marlon said he knew this spot where the trees were lovely. He had brought a saw. My goodness, we couldn't believe how handy Marlon was with that saw. One, two, three, he had that tree down. And we picked a real beauty. It is very tall and elegant. We have this argument every year. Ozzie and I favor fat bunchy trees, and Gwen and Lady like tall and elegant. Clem just likes pretty, which, she feels, can go either way. But this year I had to admit that I was like Clem, and that the prettiest tree was this slender one. It reminded me of a ballerina on tiptoe, and it wore its boughs as prettily and symmetrically as a ballerina's tutu.

I can't say we were much help in chopping it down. We all just sat there on a log sipping cocoa from the thermos Jackie had sent with us and eating molasses crinkles while Marlon did the work. But it was so much fun and we sang Christmas carols and then Marlon surprised us all. He sang one in French!! We were dumbfounded. Marlon learned French because he worked one time in a lumber camp up in northern Minnesota on the Canadian border and most of the lumberjacks were French Canadians. That's how he learned how to chop down trees so well. Lady says that Marlon sure is a good advertisement for learning without the benefit of school. I agree. Clem is just moony over him. You can tell.

We brought the tree home and decorated it while we listened to *Buck Rogers*, and Papa did come down for the radio program but he seemed sort of distracted. He sat there as if he were in a trance with a mug of cocoa in his hand and never took a sip throughout the whole program. Then he went straight upstairs. I swear I think he practically sleeps up there. Except I don't think he sleeps. His eyes look very red and his eyelids are puffy. I wonder what Marlon thinks of Papa. I want Marlon to think only good of our family but Papa is so strange lately. Not as bad as one father I read about in the paper, however. There was a story in the newspaper this morning about a man charged with disorderly conduct and the judge asked his wife what she wanted done with him, and she said that she wanted him kept in jail over the holidays so the children could have a happy Christmas. Gwen said that these times are the hardest on fathers. She says that so many are out of work and men don't know what to do with time when they are out of work. That's why you see so many tipsy downtown. Papa seems to know what to do with time. He goes upstairs but none of us knows what he's doing up there. He has a "Please Knock" sign on the door. Now, that just isn't like Papa at all.

Oh, I forgot, we ate the guinea hen for dinner. It wasn't bad. Not even a one on the vomitron. Many feathers now. We are all working like crazy on our Christmas presents.

DECEMBER 17, 1932

Gwen is a little blue, I think because she is not going to the Christmas Tinsel Time Dance. She could go even without a date but she is afraid of running into Delbert Frink. Clem is going with Marlon and Lady is going with Homer Peet. The O's are going without dates but Lady kind of shares Homer with them at dances like these. Gwen said she would take Ozzie and me and Willie Faye to the movies. There's a double feature at the Circle — *Tarzan the Ape Man* and *Horse Feathers* with the Marx Brothers. This is the only show Ozzie would agree to see. He loves Tarzan comic books, and he also thinks the Marx Brothers are the cat's whiskers.

Lady is working on Clem's outfit. She says

Clem has to stick to that tailored tuxedo look. So now you can't believe what she's doing. Papa had an old tuxedo jacket that moths got to and it was generally falling apart. Well, Lady recut the whole thing to nip in at the waist and tailored it to fit Clem. Lots of the moth holes simply disappeared because they got tucked into seams. The ones that were left weren't that bad. Then she found, in the bottom of the chest where she keeps fabric, a piece she'd bought three years before. It was a bright pink. She cut it on the bias and made a slim skirt that fell so gracefully. We were all kind of stunned. No one but Lady would ever have thought of putting pink and black together in this way. I mean, you think of pink as being a very soft, feminine color and black as being kind of mysterious and glamorous. There was just something a little shocking about it. Not in a bad way. But when Clem tried it on she looked absolutely sensational. Then Lady got the hair crimper out and heated it up on the stove. She made these soft waves in Clem's hair and then pinned one side back with a rhinestone barrette.

Lady's dress was incredible. She took an old slip. At Nick Kerz in their tree-trimming section she had bought a bunch of that silver tinsel to hang on Christmas trees, and she sewed it to the slip in overlapping rows. She sewed some to a white turban she had made to cover her chopped-off hair. She looked like she belonged on top of a Christmas tree — but not exactly as an angel. Mama said Hollywood should hire Lady. Lady is kind of a genius even though she's flunking Latin and not doing so hot in trigonometry.

We just ate beans on toast and tomato soup for supper. I love beans on toast. We're all going to the movies. Papa said Mama should go, too. I think she went just to please him although he's not going.

LATER

Papa is gone! He has left! There was a note. I cannot believe this is really happening. I can't write anymore now.

AN HOUR LATER

This IS really happening. But it still seems very unreal. When we got home from the movies, we sat down by the Christmas tree. It had begun to snow outside and we turned all the lights out in the living room and turned on the Spartan, which had Christmas music. Kate Smith was singing "O Holy Night." Then Mama got this funny look on her face, jumped up, and ran upstairs. She went first to the room on the third floor. Then we heard her coming down again to her and Papa's bedroom. Then we heard this little yelp. Gwen, Ozzie, Willie Faye, and I all jumped up and raced upstairs. Mama was standing by the bedroom door. She was holding a piece of paper. It trembled in her hands. But I was really not looking at the paper so much as I was at Mama. In the space of two minutes Mama had been transformed. It was as if she weren't Mama anymore. There was an old lady standing in front of me. She had shrunk in her dress. Her shoulders hunched and her lips moved around the shape of words that would not come. But finally they came. "Papa has left us."

"Forever?" Gwen asked.

"I don't know. He says we are not to worry. Not to worry, hah!" Mama's voice came out hot and scalding. Her lips scrolled into a hideous smirk. Mama looked like a monster. And then suddenly she just seemed to crumple up, crumple up like that piece of paper she crunched in her fist. She doubled over and sank to the floor. Gwen went to her and held her. Gwen kept saying, "It'll be all right, Mama. It'll be all right."

And Mama said, "Nothing's right. Nothing's been right for a long, long time."

Then Ozzie, trying to be helpful, but I could tell he was really scared, said, "Well, Mama, at least he didn't blast his head off like Mr. Otis." Gwen gave Ozzie a poisonous look and Willie Faye grabbed Ozzie's hand and yanked him away.

EVEN LATER

Lady and Clem came back and Marlon and Homer were with them along with the O's. Gwen had to go down and tell them. Lady asked if Gwen had read the note but Gwen said Mama just told her it said not to worry. But no one has actually read it.

I said before that this was going to be a different kind of Christmas. I sure didn't expect this, however. It truly is The Time of the Dwindling. Our family is just dwindling away. You can't replace a father. I mean, it's nice having Willie Faye here, a girl my own age. And I am awfully glad that Clem has such a nice boyfriend as Marlon. But we need a father. Not just a father. We need Papa.

DECEMBER 18, 1932

There is always this kind of funny time, I think, when you first wake up in the morning, when your head is a little bit foggy. This morning when I woke up I felt this horrible sadness. And for the first few seconds I didn't know why I felt that way, but I knew I felt it. It just lay on me like a big clammy, wet thing. Then I remembered: Papa's gone. He's left. And it was as if I had to work on it. I had to think about it and kind of nod my head and say, Yes, this is true. This is so real and at the same time unreal. Other people's fathers leave, but not ours. Now it feels like there is this big hole in our family, and I feel as if I have been snapped in two, as if I am a piece of furniture that has lost a leg or something. And this afternoon is the stupid Christmas pageant. I don't want to go at all but Mama says we must "soldier on," whatever that means.

We got to school a little bit late, and when we went backstage all of a sudden everyone stopped talking and I could tell that they were looking at me out of the corners of their eyes. Within three seconds I knew that they all knew about Papa. I whispered to Willie Faye. I said, "Willie Faye, I don't think I can do this. I've got to get out of here."

"You can't leave. Don't worry. I'll help you." If I hadn't been so upset I might have laughed. Imagine Willie Faye helping me. Willie Faye, who barely weighs sixty pounds, Willie Faye, who blew into our lives like a ball of tumbleweed, Willie Faye, who had never even seen a toilet. But I go ahead and start putting on my costume. Actually Willie Faye gave me a little push toward the rack where all the costumes hung. Then I see Martine Vontill coming toward me. She has her face all arranged in a kind of mask of pity. If there is one thing I can't stand it's pity, especially fake pity, and this is definitely fake pity. Willie Faye sees her coming and is just finishing strapping on her angel wings over her white tunic. Martine says, "Minerva, we are all so sorry to hear about your father deserting your family."

"DESERTING!" I can't believe I'm hearing that word. I can almost feel this strange little tremor pass through Willie Faye. And then I hear Willie

Faye speak, but it's not really like Willie Faye's voice. I don't know whose voice it is but it's coming out of that teensy body of hers and her tinfoil halo is kind of crooked over one eye. She says, "Martine, you are mistaken." And I see Martine kind of stiffen up. "Mr. Swift has not deserted anyone. He has been called."

"Called?" Martine says. The arrangement of fake pity on her face begins to slip away and be replaced by genuine confusion. She wasn't the only one confused, however. I had no idea what Willie Faye was talking about, and her voice . . . it was stranger than anything I ever listened to on *The Shadow*.

"We can't say anything more," Willie Faye says.

"Who called him?" Martine says, a little bit of snottiness creeping into her voice. By this time Betty and Lucy have come over. Betty turns to Martine and says, "Don't you have ears to go with that big mouth of yours, Martine? Didn't you hear Willie Faye say that she was not at liberty to speak?" Betty Hodges is really something when she gets her dander up. This was perfect.

Then Lucy jumps in. "It's obviously a mission of some sort."

Willie Faye nods, and when I saw her so did I. Martine just turned and walked off in a huff.

Martine plays the innkeeper's wife. It suits her. And I bet if she had been the innkeeper's wife back in the time of Jesus she would have turned Mary and Joseph away, too. Some people never change.

Then Mrs. Gordon came out and called, "Places, everyone! Places!" But before I went off to sleep in the heap with Lucy and Betty, I turned to Willie Faye. "Willie Faye, how'd you ever think up that story?"

"I didn't really have to think it up, Minnie."

"What do you mean?"

"I can't exactly explain. I just think it's true. Your papa wouldn't run off. He's not a running-off kind of man. I just know it."

"How do you know it, Willie Faye?"

"I just do."

"But I don't understand."

"You try too hard to understand. Your whole family does. They are just so filled up with ideas and words. It's wonderful but sometimes it just doesn't work."

"But what does work?"

She looked down at the toes of her shoes, the

ones we bought her at Stout's. She scuffed them on the floor and the feathers at the edges of her wings sort of quivered in the breeze. "I don't know. You just kind of got to believe." Willie Faye turned and starting climbing the steps to the platform that the angels stand on.

I thought about this the whole time I was in the shepherds' heap. I sure didn't think about bosoms even once, and if I had I don't think I would have laughed. When it is time for the angels to come on, they play the angel song. The lights come up and the angels in their silvery satin robes appear. Everyone in the audience always goes, "Aaaah," because it is a pretty sight. But this year you could hear them almost catch their breath. I looked up. I knew right away it was Willie Faye that made them catch their breath. She was so tiny up there but she seemed to sparkle like no other angel. And around her head, well, yes, there was the tinfoil halo but I swear there was something else. It almost looked like those little clouds of dust that puffed out of her shoes when she first arrived. But the dust wasn't dark now. It was lit by the stage lights and seemed to swirl around her head all silvery and bright. I couldn't take my eyes off Willie Faye. It was as if she were some little dust angel who had been blown out of the Texas Panhandle all the way to Indianapolis just for me and my family.

Willie Faye had said, "You just kind of got to believe," and I realized that she must have meant that we had to have faith. For what is faith but believing what you can't see. I can't see Papa right now but I believe that he did not desert us. I believe that he is on a mission. I think Willie Faye is right. Sometimes our family is just too talky, too filled up with ideas and trying to understand everything so completely, but we can believe. It's kind of like radio. We listen to all our favorite programs, *Charlie Chan*, *Buck Rogers*, *The Shadow*. Radio is funny. You can't ever see the people but you do see them in your imagination. In one way you know they aren't real, but in another way you kind of believe they are. And it is just by believing in them, real or not, that it somehow changes you inside. It's kind of like reading. You don't have to believe every book you read is real to believe that it could happen. That it is a good story.

I decided right then on stage, about three minutes before Miss Gordon got to the "Lo" part for the shepherds, that I was going to believe that Papa is on a mission. I don't care what anybody says. I am going to have faith, and that's all that counts in the end. I just marched right across the stage with my shepherd's crook and looked right into the face of that raggedy old doll that they have every year in the manger and said to myself, "I believe." And I felt Willie Faye looking down at me from the angel platform.

I didn't say anything more to Willie Faye that night about how much she had helped me. I didn't say anything to Mama or Gwen or Clem or Lady or Ozzie. I feel kind of private about this. I think maybe that faith is kind of a private thing. Or maybe it's like what Mama always says: "You can lead a horse to water but you can't make it drink."

DECEMBER 19, 1932

Mama IS soldiering on. Her face is grim and set looking, and it seems to me that she marches instead of walks around the house. But every now and then she lets her soldier's mask slip.

The wind is blowing hard now, whistling down

the chimney. The eaves creak and the windows rattle. When we were at the kitchen table there was a sudden gust that just turned the world outside white. Jackie looked out and said, "Even a colored person could get hisself lost in this." Then she realized what she had said and clapped her hand over her mouth. I saw Mama's eyes fill up with tears.

Clem jumped right up and said, "I'm going to put on some cider with cloves and cinnamon. I just love that spicy smell swirling about on a day like this." I think Clem would have said anything to change the subject.

Mama just gave this brittle smile and got up from the table and said, "I've got some Christmas secrets to work on." I can't imagine what. As a matter of fact Gwen and Clem told Mama and Papa last month that they shouldn't bother themselves with gifts for us children, that we would understand. Ozzie and I were not so sure about this. But Gwen gave us such a severe look that we didn't say anything.

We are all for that matter working on Christmas secrets and we have to work separately so we won't give away any surprises. Lady and Willie Faye are working in our bedroom, putting the finishing touches on the feather hats for Clem, Gwen, and Mama. They are also working on a plaid tie and vest for Papa. I'm going up to Papa's room to work on the decoupage boxes. Ozzie is in his lab, and Clem and the O's are in Clem's bedroom.

We haven't had any meat for days now. Not even a chicken. I told Jackie I would die if we had tuna hot dish, though. So she's making green tomato pie from the tomatoes she and Mama canned last summer. "Now, I suppose you want chocolate pudding for dessert." So I say yes, that would be very fine. "And how about some cornbread?" Oh, gosh, this could be the best dinner ever. Then I remember that we haven't made a present for Jackie. I rush upstairs to Lady and Willie Faye and tell them we have to make a hat for Jackie. All Jackie ever wears on her head when she is working in our kitchen is an old silk stocking tied up like a little beanie with her hair stuffed under it. She says it's the most sanitary way to work in a kitchen because it keeps hair and sweat out of the food. It does make her look funny, though, because Jackie has a very big round head and moon face, and when she smacks her hair down with that tight little stocking beanie, she seems rounder and more moonish. Despite being so big, it seems as if she can float around our kitchen. Jackie sort of defies gravity, as they say. Anyhow, I know that Jackie wears fancy hats to church, and Lady says that Homer Peet saw Jackie all dressed up down at the Tick Tock Club listening to Erroll Grandy, who is a jazz piano player and is as famous for jazz as Booth Tarkington is for books. And he's from right here in Indianapolis. So she would have times to wear this hat and not just to church.

LATER

Ozzie is not doing very well. He's been really quiet. Then tonight he came into our bedroom. He just blurted it all out. "I think Papa's dead."

Willie Faye was so shocked she stood right up on the bed. "He's not dead, Ozzie. He's not. I just know it." Ozzie looked so miserable. I told him to listen to Willie Faye because I thought Willie Faye was right about Papa not just up and leaving or "just vanishing," as Ozzie keeps saying. Then Willie Faye said the most amazing thing. "Your Papa has not vanished. He is somewhere. He knows where he is. We don't." Ozzie and I both blinked. There was a strange kind of logic here. It seemed to jolt Ozzie out of his misery just a bit.

So then he climbed up on Willie Faye's bed and asked for a story — the one about the cut-off cows' heads. But Willie Faye just sighed and said that she had told him that story at least seventeen times and she didn't want to tell it any-more. She'd tell him another story. A Christmas Eve story. So she told him one. It was THE BEST. I can't believe the adventures that Willie Faye had out in that emptiness called Heart's Bend, Texas. And Willie Faye is a great storyteller. This was something that happened the second time in her life that Willie Faye saw snow. I am going to try to write it down here just the way she told it. I am going to say "I" just as if it were Willie Faye speaking. Here's what Willie Faye told:

"It was Christmas Eve. The wind shrieked like a pack of coyotes, driving the snow so hard that it drifted over the windows. Every now and then the chimney would suck down a huge draft and burp out puffs of ash right into the room. It was a night when you knew that every ani-mal out on the range — the winter jackrabbit, the red fox,

the titmouse — had all burrowed in. But Daddy had to go out, not far, no more than twenty feet from the house, to check on the cattle in the pens. Two were due to drop calves. Well, when he came back in he was like to be tied. The wind had blown down part of the fencing and one of the cows had got out. He was going to have to go and find her. If she gave birth out there on the open range both she and the calf would freeze to death.

'Long about midnight I started to worry because Daddy wasn't back. I thought maybe I'd just peek out the door. I could see dim marks where Daddy had walked. I grabbed my big boots, put on Mama's coat, wrapped three scarves around my head, and set out.

It was pretty easy at first, following the footprints, but suddenly the wind came up and a wall of snow blew in. The whole world turned white. I didn't know what was up and what was down. I had heard cowboys talk about this. They called them whiteouts and they are very dangerous.

Now, you're not going to believe this but I was even littler then than I am now, and I suddenly felt myself picked up in a huge whoosh. I was flying through the air, tumbling this way and that and then I just dropped. I dropped onto something warm and furry but a little bit wet. Then I heard this bellow. It was my daddy. "Willie Faye!"

123

"Daddy!" I said. We both just stared at each other. Then I realized that I had landed right on the rump of the cow.

Daddy said, "I thought I just delivered this here calf but it seems like something delivered you as well." I looked down, and sure enough, I saw something shiny, shiny as polished river stones. It was the calf's eyes staring up at me and there was a little frozen teardrop in the corner of one eye.

It was the cutest little calf you ever did see. Then Daddy said we had to hurry up and figure out how to keep us all warm, because there was no finding our way back in that whiteout. Daddy had already begun to pile up snow into a windbreak. He told me that that was how the Eskimos made their igloos and that if we piled up enough, the four of us could stay warm.

And it was funny the way he said "the four of us." It was as if we were all one family. There wasn't any separation between people and animals. There were just some creatures that were mothers and fathers and others that were little children. I had heard those stories about the magical Christmas Eve when at midnight the animals could talk. We weren't exactly speaking out loud to one another but we all knew what the others were thinking.

We got the windbreak built and crowded in around the heifer with the calf at her teat.

Pretty soon it stopped snowing. We looked up and the sky was prickly with stars. And Daddy started to point out the constellations. I saw Orion stumbling up there with his club and the lion skin he holds. Daddy told me all the stories that went with the star pictures. And I think the heifer and the calf were listening, too. The sky that night was prettier than any Christmas tree. It was as if every star, every constellation was getting out of its cloudy bed to give us creatures on earth this spectacle. I could look into the black shiny eye of the calf and see the stars reflected. And there really were no separations amongst God's creatures and there was nothing dividing us from the stars. When I looked into that calf's eye and saw the stars I thought, The stars are in us and we are in the stars.

Come morning, the sun broke out and with Daddy carrying the calf and me leading the heifer, we walked home. I wanted to bring the calf right in by the fire and the heifer, too. I wanted us all to be together on this Christmas morning, but Daddy and Mama said no. I guess the magic was over. The separations were back and it was time for animals to be with animals and people with people.

VERY LATE

We were real quiet for the longest time after Willie Faye finished telling her story. "You know, it's stopped snowing outside," Willie Faye said finally. "Maybe we could go see if there are any star pictures. The winter constellations should be up."

We'd have to go up on the flat part of the roof to see them and that was sort of against the rules, but we figured that Mama was so distracted about Papa that she wouldn't notice. It was my idea to bring the peaches and some molasses crinkles to eat. Ever since I ate peaches outside in the snow I think it's really the only way to have them. So I put the peaches jar in a basket, and three bowls and spoons, and tied the cookies up in a napkin, and we went up to the third floor and crawled out through a window onto the flat part of the roof. Ozzie has brought his telescope and he sets it up. Willie Faye has never in her life looked through a telescope and she is just about knocked over by what she sees. It is all so clear and seems so close. I nearly laugh when I see her reach out her hand as if she plans to touch a star. But Ozzie is still very quiet. Normally he would be jabbering on about Saturn's rings or Magellanic Clouds or galaxies.

But he is so quiet it gives me the creeps. He's just standing there on the rooftop, staring out into space. I'm not sure but it is almost as if he is looking for something in particular. Then finally he says to Willie Faye without even turning around to speak to her, "Willie Faye, when you flew it was kind of like magic, wasn't it? I mean you were blown right to where your Daddy was." It was then I knew what poor Ozzie was thinking about. He was thinking about Papa and he was hoping that maybe some kind of weird Christmas magic would just all of a sudden blow Papa back to us.

DECEMBER 20, 1932

The O's are coming over this afternoon with Opal's cousin. Opal's cousin was in World War I and he is missing a hand. It got blown off at the battle of Verdun in France. Clem has warned us at least thirty-five times not to stare. I have a feeling Ozzie won't be able to hold back from staring.

Ozzie stared, all right. Clem kept clearing her throat and coughing. Finally I said, "You're getting a cold." I found her constant gargling worse than Ozzie's staring. But Opal's cousin, his name is Harry, didn't seem to notice. He was talking about Hoover and how awful the veterans' march was in Washington last summer. He was in it. More than twenty thousand veterans marched in Washington to demand their bonuses from serving in World War I. They had been promised these bonuses from Congress and now so many of them were out of work, they were going hungry and their families were, too. They camped out in tents and built shacks right in the city of Washington, D.C. But President Hoover wouldn't listen to them and then, worse than that, he turned the police on them! Turned the police on the very men who had fought across the seas to keep the world safe for democracy. I remember Papa saying that when That Fool Hoover did that, he lost the election even though the election would not be for a few more months.

Harry is very nice, but he has sadness about him. He's old. Over thirty! And he's been married but his wife died. He's lost a lot—his hand, his wife, and his job last spring. He's come to live with Opal and her family for a while. Marlon is going to see about getting him a job at Ayres. If anyone can do it, it's Marlon.

I wish Marlon could do something about Papa. I guess that is asking too much. I keep trying to believe the way Willie Faye told me to. It's hard. And I can't believe for Mama. I can see that Mama is not able to hide her worry so well. Soldiering on is getting harder.

Speaking of soldiering on, there was a picture of Mrs. Roosevelt in the paper today going into a coal mine in West Virginia and then another one of her in the same town shaking hands with little dirty-faced children. It reminded me of the little boy we saw in the shantytown, the one who asked me if his cookie through Christmas magic might turn into Santa Claus.

Ozzie said the weirdest thing this evening. He said, "I wonder what Al Capone is doing for Christmas." Al Capone—the biggest gangster ever and Ozzie is wondering whether he's going to have a nice Christmas in jail!

Gwen was allowed to bring family members to the Bobbs-Merrill publishing company Christmas party last night. Ozzie and Mama didn't want to go but Clem, Willie Faye, Lady, and I all went. I must admit that I was a little worried that they'd have lots of aspic from that *Joy of Cooking* book. But they didn't and it was a really nice party with punch, every sort of cookie imaginable, and a turkey and a ham. I wish Mama and Ozzie had come. Willie Faye and I got dressed up. Lady cut down an old party dress of mine for Willie Faye. It was plaid with velvet trim and we found matching bows for her hair. I wore a sailor dress. I don't generally like sailor dresses but it was all that fit me and Mama likes it, and I just didn't want to put up a fuss when she's feeling so bad. As Lady said, "So, darn it, you'll go as a sailor." The party was nice and they gave each of us a present. They publish a lot of children's books. They gave Willie Faye a copy of *Raggedy Ann*. I think they thought she was a lot younger than she is. They gave me a book from the Childhood of Famous Americans series. George Washington. It's all right. It didn't thrill me. In a way I would rather read about the childhood of unfamous Americans — just normal kids who lived through something like the Civil War or the Revolutionary War.

I did meet Mr. John Jay Curtis, who is a company officer and according to Gwen is supersmart and thinks up what she calls sales strategy. When he asked me how I liked the book I said fine, but then I told him I thought they should have more girls in the series. He said, "Well, we're going to be doing Martha Washington and Betsy Ross."

I didn't want to say this but I think a book on Betsy Ross might be a colossal bore. Instead I said, "How about one on Amelia Earhart?"

There was another lady standing next to him and she looked kind of shocked. And then she said the stupidest thing I ever heard. "But she's so modern. She can't really be considered history yet."

Well, I just blurted out, "She IS history. You don't have to be dead to be interesting. What could be more interesting than being the first woman to fly solo across the Atlantic Ocean?"

Now the lady really looked shocked. "My goodness, aren't you a pert young lady." I didn't mind the pert part, but I HATE HATE HATE it when grownups call girls "young ladies." All it really means is that we're teensy and powerless and don't know our place. Well, maybe I don't know my place but I know what's history and what's interesting. But the good part is that Mr. Curtis didn't seem to be paying attention to her. He raised his eyebrows and said, "Now, Minerva, that's not a half-bad idea."

LATER

I keep on thinking about Amelia Earhart. I got out my scrapbook and showed Willie Faye the pictures of her I had cut out from the newspaper when she made her flight last May. Guess what Willie Faye says. She says I look just like Amelia Earhart. You know, I think she's right. If I cut my hair shorter and wore bangs that are just a little puffy on top I would look like her.

ONE HOUR LATER

I look almost exactly like Amelia Earhart except shorter. Lady cut my hair. This is so exciting. Now Clem jokes that I better learn how to fly. She jokes, but why not?

. . .

Holy smokes! Marlon knows how to fly a plane. He flies a biplane out at a little airport in Carmel. He said he would take me for a ride. Mama said, "Yee gads! Over my dead body." Gosh, what a spoilsport she is. If she weren't so worried about Papa I would really put up a fight over this. When I put my mind to it I can whine like nobody's business. I've been known to drive every one of my sisters out of the house with whining. Jackie says I could whine the feathers off a chicken. For some reason my whining doesn't get to Ozzie.

Not much gets to Ozzie these days. He didn't even come down to listen to *The Shadow* tonight. So I went upstairs to look for him and where did I find him but on the roof looking out, just the way he was the other night—hoping, I guess, that Papa will be blown back to us the way Willie Faye was blown to her daddy. A part of me wishes Willie Faye had never told us that story.

DECEMBER 22, 1932

This morning Willie Faye and I went over to Betty Hodges's with Lucy, and we built a snowman, and a snowwoman, too. When we came inside to get warm, Mrs. Hodges had made cocoa for us. I like Mrs. Hodges a lot but she kept looking at me with these very sad eyes. I know that she was thinking, Oh, poor child, her father's gone off and left the family. I just know she was thinking that. She was looking at me like I was some half orphan. I hate being looked at that way. So I snatched off my knit hat and I said to Mrs. Hodges, "Don't you think I look like Amelia Earhart with my hair short?"

She kind of snapped out of it and said, "Why my goodness, Minerva, you do bear a striking resemblance to her." She was all right after that. No more sappy, teary little looks. I swear sometimes you really have to shape up these grown-ups, be a little strict with them.

LATER

I can't believe I never noticed it but after we got back from Betty Hodges's I went upstairs to Papa's room. I had been working on my Christmas gifts for at least an hour when I saw that his typewriter was missing! Now I can't remember seeing it when I was up here yesterday, either. Whatever has happened to it? Mama was going to the Fortnightly afternoon tea today. I'll ask her when she comes back.

LATER

This is unbelievable. Mama did not go to the Fortnightly afternoon tea. She and Ozzie went downtown to hire a private detective to look for Papa. And what did she use for money? She sold the typewriter! And this is almost more unbelievable: Ozzie sold his chemistry set to Homer Peet's younger brother Chester. Mama swears that she did not make Ozzie sell his set, that he had already done it and that she would have come up with the difference between what the typewriter brought and the cost of hiring a detective. This is all so incredible. I mean, people like us don't hire private detectives. We are the Swifts. We are a very boring, predictable (until Papa up and left) normal family. I am trying to imagine Lamont Cranston or Charlie Chan showing up here at our house, 4605 North Meridian Street. We are becoming a radio show! Or at least like one. I picture Charlie Chan in our kitchen interviewing Jackie. It boggles the brain.

I guess it can't do any harm and there is one good thing: Ozzie seems a lot happier. He keeps saying, "Well, at least we're doing something to find Papa."

DECEMBER 23, 1932

Gwen has today off and is taking us all to lunch at the Ayres tearoom. She got a very generous Christmas bonus from Bobbs-Merrill, and she said that in any case she gets a company discount at Ayres so she can afford to take us to lunch. Ayres is my favorite place to go for lunch. I always have the same thing: chicken à la king, hot chocolate in a clown mug with whipped cream and sprinkles on top, and three-colored Jell-O for dessert with a sugar cookie. Mama doesn't want to go. Ozzie says Ayres tearoom is a sissy place. But I know that both he and Mama want to stay home in case Mr. Fromeyer calls. Mr. Fromeyer is the detective. I don't think Fromeyer is a very detective-sounding name.

LATER

We were all trying very hard to be merry down at the tearoom, but maybe it wasn't such a good idea to go because we saw lots of families with mothers and fathers and I guess we did feel a little incomplete. The chicken à la king didn't taste quite the same and at least two of Mama's friends from the Fortnightly Club and one from the Woman's Club came over to see how we were doing. You knew exactly what they really wanted to say: "Any word from your father?"

There were fashion models in the tearoom that sashayed around the tables in dresses and gowns from the French Room, the most expensive department in Ayres. But I don't know who can afford to wear these clothes anymore. Gwen says they just show a few of the fancy ones for entertainment — like the movies. It kind of distracts you to see something glamorous. And it was as if these models weren't quite real. They could have been up there on a movie screen. I mean, what are they going to model? Hoover blankets? One model sort of slithered up to our table and said, "Good afternoon, ladies. I am wearing an ensemble by Monsieur Montaldo. It is tiers of chiffon overlaying a bias-cut skirt with this lovely evening coat trimmed in white fox. Isn't it perfect for the holiday season?" And we all nodded. Yes, it was perfect, and I think every one of us pictured Mama in it. Mama has such a nice slender figure she would have looked lovely in it. Most of the ladies eating lunch, like the ones who came over to ask how we were doing, were "portly," as Clem says. I say "fat," but Clem says that is not a polite word. Fat is fat as far as I'm concerned. It is not a question of being polite. All these ladies had their fat laced in or hooked in or zippered up with corsets. Mama doesn't even wear a corset.

After lunch we went to Charlie Mayer's. They have the most elegant gifts in the world. Willie Faye's and my favorite things were the snow babies. They are tiny china figures that can be hung on Christmas trees. We loved the one of a baby riding a polar bear. Our other favorite thing was a cuckoo clock that played "We Three Kings" and then the Wise Men popped out, each holding his gift for the baby Jesus. That clock cost three hundred dollars! But it's just like the models and the clothes: Who is going to buy a three-hundred-dollar clock or even a snow baby that costs eight dollars? But there were scads of people pressing up against the glass at Charles Mayer's.

Sometimes when I think about this Great Depression I think that there has never been such a collision between realness and fantasy. It is as if we are standing with our feet in the muck and grime of these hard times but our noses are pressed up against the window of some fantastically glamorous world. These times are so strange. And that reminds me. Mama is talking about shutting down another room — her and Papa's bedroom. She says that as long as Papa's not here she might as well sleep in with Clem and Gwen. What if the winter is really long and cold? Where will we get enough money for coal?

When we got home Ozzie wasn't there. Lucky boy! Mr. Jasper, who is Jackie's gentleman friend and owns the best barbecue place in town, had come by in his Hudson and driven them over to Indiana Avenue to have lunch. Mama wouldn't go, of course. But Ozzie did. Jasper's B'Cue, unlike the tearoom, is no sissy place. There are pinball machines, on Saturday nights they have a jazz trio, and they serve the best catfish in the state of

Indiana. Ozzie ate seven catfish!! Catfish aren't that big but I bet he ate almost two pounds. Then he had pecan pie and Coca-Cola, which Mama would die if she heard he had a Coca-Cola. She thinks Coca-Cola is the worst thing in the world for children. Anyhow, you can bet that at Jasper's there were no white ladies in corsets with sappy eyes being nosey about Papa.

I can't quite believe that it is December 23, that tomorrow is Christmas Eve, and that there still is no word from Papa. Whatever can he be thinking? He has a whole family waiting and worrying and wondering, and it is only two days until Christmas. It is very hard believing. I almost get mad at Willie Faye. I want to say, How do you know about any of this? How do you know what it's like for us? But then I realize that she does know a lot. Willie Faye is a real, genuine orphan. She has seen a dead body, her mama's. She had to live in the same house with it for two days. No, Willie Faye has seen a lot. I can't really get mad at her.

I've finished wrapping all my Christmas presents. Mama said that this year we have no money for fancy wrapping paper and ribbons, so we have to be inventive. Well, I used the funny papers for lots of my presents, and then Willie Faye got this great idea of using scraps of material from Lady's fabric chest. I made the decoupage boxes look really pretty by tying them up in pink satin, and then I found a lovely piece of red cut velvet that is more beautiful than any Christmas wrapping paper. Lady said it was fine for us to use the scraps.

Opal's cousin Harry came by today. Lady and I think he might be sweet on Gwen. How will they hold hands? Well, I guess he still has one she could hold but she'll always have to get on the right side. It could be awkward. Still, even with one hand he is a thousand times better than Delbert Frink.

DECEMBER 24, 1932
EARLY MORNING

I can't believe this is the day of Christmas Eve. I don't even want to get up. I mean, how am I — how are we — ever going to get through this day and tomorrow? I just can't imagine us hanging up our stockings or sitting around the Christmas tree. Clem is going caroling with the O's. They invited Willie Faye and me to tag along, but I can't imagine singing. I think I'll start crying. When I think about Papa I picture him in some shantytown like Curtisville Bottom. I imagine him standing over an oil drum burning with coals, warming his hands with some hobos. I wonder if he's become a hobo and is riding the rails somewhere. How could he give us up for that? I'm not supposed to think this way. I am not supposed to give up. I have to try to believe like Willie Faye said to. I heard Mama on the phone in the upstairs hall with Mr. Fromeyer. It didn't sound promising. Just lots of sighs from Mama and the occasional, "Oh, well." This guy is no Dick Tracy. I hear a lot of commotion down-stairs. I better get up.

TWENTY MINUTES LATER

The commotion was Marlon and Harry. They arrived with a live turkey for our Christmas dinner tomorrow. Jackie's going to kill it now. Willie Faye ran down to tell her to save the feathers and not scald them off because that ruins them. I don't know how Marlon and Harry got hold of this turkey, but they did. Now Marlon says we are all to put on our warmest clothes. We're going to go skating and sledding. We don't have any ice skates that will fit Willie Faye but she can sled.

LATE AFTERNOON

We did have fun out at Lake Sullivan. Marlon is the most beautiful ice skater. Harry isn't bad, either. And he didn't need any help lacing up his skates even though he only has one hand. Willie Faye and I went double on the Flexible Flyer and then Homer Peet had his toboggan and six of us went down the big hill on that. We usually bring marshmallows and roast them. But no one dared ask Mama for money for marshmallows. I guess I got as jolly as I could get, considering the circumstances. I worried, though, about Mama and Ozzie. Ozzie refused to come. At least Jackie is at home with them. She and Mama were going to start cooking the Christmas dinner today. I think there is going to be a lot of au gratins. Ozzie says he hopes they don't "gratinize" the turkey that Marlon brought to make it go further. Mama had this really fierce look on her face when I asked her if she was going to make the mincemeat pies. "Of course!" she barked. "This is going to be Christmas as usual."

Well, I didn't argue with her and Gwen gave me a look that said I better not even think about opening my mouth. But this is not going to be Christmas as usual. And you don't have to be Albert Einstein to figure that out.

We never do anything very grand for Christmas Eve dinner, and this year it is especially so. Jackie made a big noodle casserole and fried up the last of the green tomatoes. There was Waldorf salad with chopped apples and nuts, and my favorite — chocolate pudding. Christmas dinner is much fancier. Sweet potatoes stuffed in hollowed-out oranges and topped with melted marshmallows, but no marshmallows this year and no oranges. I think the sweet potatoes are going to look a little naked on the plate. And we always have a three-colored Jell-O mold. Ozzie says Jell-O is really cheap so we'll still probably have that. But tonight I was kind of staring down at my plate thinking that I was glad that the food wasn't fancy. Without Papa it would be so hard looking at all the Christmas food. And what will we do tomorrow? I wasn't even really hungry. Then I noticed that absolutely no one was talking. There was dead silence around the table. I looked up and everybody was just like me, staring at the food on their plates. Then Lady said, "I'm not really that hungry." And she pushed away her plate.

"Me neither," said Ozzie and sank back in his chair.

Clem suddenly stood up. "I think we should all go over to Curtisville and take this food. None of us is hungry, or maybe we just don't have the heart to eat. But we shouldn't waste this food."

Everyone thinks this is a terrific idea except for me. You see, I am afraid that maybe Papa is living over there. Maybe we will run into him.

"What about the caroling?" I asked.

"We can carol over there," Clem said. "I'll call Marlon and he'll bring his car and with two cars we can all fit in. You'll go, won't you, Mama?"

"Of course I'll go," Mama said and squared her shoulders. The soldier is back!

I'll write more later. I wonder if we'll hang up our stockings when we get back from Curtisville. I wonder if we'll even feel like hanging up our stockings.

I don't think I'll be able to write hard enough, fast enough, or maybe it should be slow enough to tell what has happened. We went to Curtisville and delivered our food, and the people were very happy and then we all sang Christmas carols and Mama sang, too. She really did more than soldier on. Willie Faye and I told her about the little boy with the dirty face that we had given the Santa Claus cookie to before and she said, "Well, let's go find him, girls." But we couldn't find him or any of his family. We found the tire house that Marlon had made safer for his family, but another family was living in it now and nobody seemed to know where they had gone. It started to snow really hard and Marlon said we had better be getting home because he was worried that the roads might turn slippery. Gwen was driving the Packard and she hasn't had much experience driving in snow.

We all piled in and said good-bye to the people who had come out to thank us once more. One old lady grabbed Mama's hand. Her fingers looked like claws and the knuckles were the size of marbles. She was almost bent double, but she came out from the little tar paper hut where she lived with her son who had a problem, she said, with "the drink." I think she meant whiskey. She said to Mama, "God bless you, lady. May only goodness come your way." And I saw Mama's eyes fill up with tears. I couldn't help but think that Mama could become this lady in a few years. What will we do if Papa never comes back? How will we live? I tried to imagine all of us stuffed into one little tar paper house.

I climbed into the Packard with Gwen and Mama and Willie Faye. Clem and Lady and Ozzie went in Marlon's car. We were all very quiet driving home. I think we were all thinking the same thought. Right now, in this hour of the year 1932, we are still better off than all those people in Curtisville. But how long will it last? And I was thinking that it surely is stupid to hang up our Christmas stockings and maybe it was even stupid to have a tree. That is the last thing I remember clearly thinking. I say "clearly" on purpose. Because what happened as soon as we drove up to the house now seems like bright bits and pieces of colored glass jiggling around in a kaleidoscope.

When we began to walk up the drive, through the frosty windows I could see that something inside the house looked different. It seemed dimmer but at the same time I could see what appeared to be a lot of candles. Everyone seemed to notice it at once. Mama said, "I could have sworn that I left the dining room light on. And what happened to the porch light? It's off, too."

Then Lady said, "Look, Mama, don't the walls look funny?"

It was almost as if we were afraid to go into our own house. We all crunched through the snow, which had gotten deep. At that moment through a side window I could see the mantel over the fireplace. "Mama! Our stockings have been hung up." We all crowded up to the side window of the living room and gasped. Not only had our stockings been hung up, with one for Willie Faye as well, but also someone had woven together pine boughs. The walls of the living room were covered with them. It was as if a magical forest had grown in our living room. And on every table candles were lit and glowed softly, their light pale and golden. Marlon whistled low.

"What's happened?" Ozzie whispered. And for the first time in his life I think Ozzie really didn't know, didn't have a clue about what was going on. I heard this voice in my head. *"You just kind of got to believe. You try too hard to understand. Your whole family does. They are just so filled up with ideas and words."* It was what Willie Faye had said at the Christmas pageant except I could hear it clearly now. I looked to see if she was really speaking. But she wasn't. Her face seemed to sparkle just like it had when she stood up on the angel platform. Now snow swirled around her head just like a halo and some flakes lighted down on her eyelashes. It was Willie Faye who led the way up the walk and was first at the door.

"Willie Faye," Mama said, "you'll need a key."

"Oh, no," Willie Faye said softly and she pushed the door open. We all went inside. There was the smell of warm candles and cinnamon and fresh pine. The Spartan glowed in the dark and Kate Smith was singing "O Holy Night" in a voice so beautiful you thought she was an angel. The stockings were not only hung but filled. There were candy canes, and small presents gaily wrapped, poking out. In one, in Mama's, a beautiful gold chain with a heart hung over the edge. The big wing chair had been pulled up to the fire. Suddenly we heard a voice. "Oh, my goodness. You caught me snoozing."

It was Papa! He stood up. He was the most welcome, wonderful sight I had ever seen. Forget about angels. He was our real life Papa. Clean shaven, eyes sparkling as they used to. He was dressed in a new shirt and his favorite tie and his old plaid bedroom slippers. "Merry Christmas, children. Merry Christmas, Belle — love of my life." And he walked toward her and embraced her and then we all just flung ourselves on Papa. He teetered a bit toward the Spartan. "Oh, for heaven's sake!" He laughed. "Let's not crash into the Spartan or else how will we listen?"

And that is how he told us. Papa had gone all the way to Chicago, to the offices of the National Broadcasting System. And our Papa had sold them three scripts for a radio program called *Ozzie, the Boy Wonder*, the stories of a boy who makes contact with life in space! That is what he was doing up there in the room on the third floor every day he came home early. K-chirp! K-chirp! The typewriter! It suddenly hit me. "But Mama sold the typewriter!" I blurted out.

"You did what, Belle?"

"Sam, I sold the typewriter. I thought you never used it and I needed the money."

"What for?"

"I hired a private detective. I was so worried, Sam."

"And I sold the chemistry set," Ozzie said.

"I didn't want him to, Sam, but you don't know how desperate we were."

"Oh, Belle. I said I'd be back. I said hold on." Papa stopped a minute. "I would have told you where I was going and what I was up to but I wasn't sure if I could sell it. I didn't want to raise anybody's hopes. But now I have sold it. Belle, they gave me six hundred dollars."

Six hundred dollars! That was more money than any of us had ever even dreamed about. Six hundred dollars! Why, Papa didn't make that much in a single month as head accountant for Greenhandle's. "But I have to write three more stories fast."

Gwen said she could borrow a typewriter for him from Bobbs-Merrill.

And then we all started laughing and crying and nobody was tired enough to go to bed, so we opened our stockings. Papa had brought back the most wonderful gifts for all of us. A necklace for Mama, a slide rule for Ozzie. A locket and chain for me and a bracelet with a glass heart for Willie Faye. A pretty hair comb for Gwen with tiny gold stars on it. For Lady, black lace gloves that went up to her elbows. For Clem, a book of poems.

After we opened our stockings we still weren't tired, so we thought why not give out the rest of the presents. Everyone loved the hats that Willie Faye and I made. We had secretly made one for Lady in addition to the earrings. And Willie Faye loved my decoupage box. She ran right up and got her pumpkin seeds and the picture from the newspaper and put them in it along with some hair ribbons and a lovely set of barrettes that Mama got her. Ozzie went wild over what Clem got him. It was a poster from that movie *Freak* that they closed down. She said that Marlon got it for her because he knew the ticket taker at the theater where it had played. Clem made me a scrapbook of Amelia Earhart with pictures and newspaper stories and then at the end, I couldn't believe it, an autographed picture of her signed to me. She had found out where to write to Miss Earhart and written and asked her for it. The picture says, "For Minerva Swift — dare to dream. Best wishes, Amelia Earhart." I could scarcely believe it. Lady had made me a replica of the flight jacket Amelia Earhart had worn and a canvas flight helmet. Gwen had bought me a pair of goggles. This will be perfect for sledding even if I can't pilot a plane yet.

But I have to say that the best presents of all were from Willie Faye. Willie Faye had made each of us a picture book. Each book was different and had a different story that she had told us. Mine was the story of the calf being born in the blizzard. For Ozzie she had illustrated the cattle rustling story and for Lady the pumpkin one. For Clem she did a book on a tornado that she had told us about, and for Gwen she did one about the worst dust storm of all when she found Tumbleweed in a three-foot pile of dust and had to suck the dirt from his nose and ears. The drawing was pretty funny. For Mama and Papa she told the story of how she had come here on the train to Indianapolis, and she had made the best picture of Mama bending down to kiss her. She even got in the part about going to Stout's for her new pair of shoes. She used colored pencils and watercolors. She worked on them most of the time in school in

Miss Morse's art class. Mama says these books are "absolute treasures."

Right now it is two o'clock in the morning, Christmas morning, and we have all finally gone to bed. We really didn't want to because it is so beautiful in the living room. We had nearly forgotten to ask Papa how he had put up all that greenery and where he got it. Well, this was another surprise. It was Onesy, our old friend the hobo with one eye, one tooth, and missing a finger, who helped him. Papa had wanted him to stay the night and join us for Christmas dinner but Onesy disappeared. Papa snapped his fingers and said, "Just vanished like that!"

But I am so happy, it is unimaginable. No, it is imaginable. I am so happy that I would gladly eat aspic for Christmas dinner tomorrow, or rather today. . . .

DECEMBER 25 — CHRISTMAS DAY!

I have never slept so late — none of us has on Christmas morning — but then I smelled bacon frying and heard a shout. Willie Faye and I raced downstairs to see what was happening. There was Jackie and Mr. Jasper standing in our kitchen. And Papa at the stove frying bacon! In an apron! I don't know what shocked Jackie more — the fact that Papa was back or that he was standing there in an apron. Jackie was holding the most beautiful chicken. They made a pretty strange picture, standing there in the kitchen. We told Jackie how Papa had come back and how he'd sold his radio show about Ozzie, the Boy Wonder, and Ozzie said, "There's going to be Martians in the third episode, Jackie."

Jackie said, "Them Martians ain't going to be any weirder than what's right here before my eyes." And she looked straight at Papa, who was now flipping pancakes. "Little green men, shoot! I never thought I'd live to see a white man in an apron out in the kitchen frying bacon and flipping jacks." This to Jackie was science fiction.

Well, then Mama and Gwen came in. They were both wearing their feather hats. Next came Lady and Clem. They were wearing their hats, too. Jackie clutched her chicken harder. "They gonna turn you into a hat, darlin'?" Then I remembered the present we'd made for Jackie, so I ran upstairs. As soon as I brought it down Jackie said, "Oh, my word!" And she shoved that hen into Mr. Jasper's arms and put the hat on. She really looked terrific. We didn't hear another sorry word about chicken and hats. As a matter of fact Jackie just turned and said, "Jasper, darlin', you take that hen out to the garage and put her with those other chickens where she belongs."

LATER

I'll never forget this Christmas. Mama invited Jackie and Mr. Jasper to stay for dinner and Marlon came, too. There were eleven of us crowded around the table. And all the girls and Mama and Jackie wore their feather hats. I looked around the table at happy faces. Then I began thinking of all the really peculiar gifts we had made and exchanged. I thought of the Wise Men, the Magi, who brought the gifts to the baby Jesus. They say it was the Magi who invented the art of giving Christmas presents. I suppose that is right, but the Swift family along with Willie Faye have sort of reinvented this art of giving gifts in the year of this Great Depression, in the year 1932. I looked at Willie Faye and I think maybe it's not just gifts we have reinvented, maybe it was belief. Willie Faye looked right back at me when I was thinking this. It was as if she knew what I might be thinking and she smiled softly.

It's funny but I shall always from now on think of my life as *before* the time Willie Faye came and *after* the time Willie Faye came. Before she came, I have to say, life seemed a little bit dull in spite of having three sisters who could yak your ears off and a brother who is inventing a way to listen for Martians and once blew up a trash can. In a funny way I'm thinking that Willie Faye, quiet as she is and in spite of not knowing before she came here what a toilet or a porcelain tub looked like, or what an adjective was, or who Charlie Chan or Booth Tarkington are, is sort of like one of those Wise Men from the Bible. She is kind of a fourth Magi. She blew in here on the skirts of a dust storm from a place called Heart's Bend, Texas, and all she had was her cat, Tumbleweed, a straw suitcase with hardly enough clothes, a cigar box of colored pencils, a photograph of herself with the biggest pumpkin in Texas, pumpkin seeds, and the wildest stories I've ever heard.

It is the Great Depression and we have stood

for a long time with our feet in the muck and the grime with our noses pressed up against the window, but tonight it was as if we just melted right through that window. And it wasn't a world of glamour and fantasy. It was home and it was warm and it felt safe. And Papa doesn't look like Clark Gable, and Mama, even though she is pretty, doesn't look like Greta Garbo. And Lady's hair is still funny and I swear I still sometimes see dust puffing out of Willie Faye's socks. And I just think that before Willie Faye came I could hardly believe that we could have a Christmas at all, but Willie Faye helped me believe — believe that Papa would come back, believe that he indeed had a mission, believe that somehow, someway, things would turn out all right and in fact it has. We have had Christmas after all.

EPILOGUE

On January 6, 1933, the twelfth day of Christmas, the celebration of the Epiphany and the Feast of the Kings, *Ozzie, the Boy Wonder* debuted on the Wild Oats Five Star Theater series. Wild Oats, a breakfast cereal company, sponsored a different half-hour show in the same slot five nights a week. Within a month *Ozzie, the Boy Wonder* was their most popular show. Within the next two years there were Ozzie comic books and then an Ozzie movie. The Swifts became very wealthy. They were able to pay Jackie a handsome wage. Gwen was able to return to college and every single one of the girls, including Willie Faye, completed their college education.

On March 4, 1933, Franklin Delano Roosevelt was inaugurated as president of the United States and began laying the groundwork to help the nation recover from the Depression. But it would not be that many years after the Depression that World War II would break out in 1939.

Some of the Swift children had completed their education by the time America entered World War II in 1941, but Minnie and Willie Faye had not. All of their lives were affected by the war. In some cases college degrees were put off; in others marriage and children were delayed.

Minnie had indeed learned how to fly by the time of the war and joined the Army Air Force, a division of women pilots. With the need abroad for combat pilots there were not enough pilots left within the United States to provide support services. Minnie, having learned how to fly on her fifteenth birthday, joined up in 1941 upon turning twenty years old. This organization was soon consolidated into the Women's Air Force Service Pilots, or WASPS, as they were known. It was a very selective organization and of the more than 25,000 applicants only 2,000 were accepted and 1,074 graduated. Minnie was one of them. Throughout the war Minnie flew a variety of assignments, including the towing of targets for air-to-air and anti-aircraft gunnery practice, engineering testing, ferrying aircraft, and other assignments.

Ozzie actually graduated early from college, having skipped the eighth grade, and entered high school as a sophomore. He went to the Massachusetts Institute of Technology and at the completion of his degree in physics, was sent to Los Alamos, New Mexico, to work on the atom bomb. After Hiroshima, Ozzie devoted himself to working on disarmament and taught at the Princeton Institute of Advanced Studies. He married a Jewish girl who was a concert violinist and a survivor of the German concentration camp Auschwitz.

Lady graduated from the Parsons School of Design in New York City and later became a costume designer for Broadway musicals. She eventually moved to Hollywood. In 1950 she received an Academy Award for the costume designs of the movie *Some Gal*. She never married but had many boyfriends even into her eighties.

After completing college, Gwen returned to Indianapolis and worked at the Bobbs-Merrill Company, where she was promoted to editor. She got tired of editing the endless editions of *Joy of Cooking* and wound up in the juvenile department editing children's books. She married Harry Knox, who completed a law degree in night school and began a law firm that specialized in legal work for war veterans. They had three children.

Clementine received a master's degree in social work and became the director of an orphanage outside of Indianapolis. She and Marlon married after a lengthy courtship. Marlon became one of Indianapolis's leading businessmen. Pursuing his idea that the highest profit margin came from nonessential but amusing items, he began a small toy manufacturing company and then diversified into several other children's products.

Willie Faye went to the John Herron Art Institute in Indianapolis and began work as an art director at the Bobbs-Merrill Company. She later began to illustrate stories and became one of America's most beloved children's book illustrators. She and Minnie collaborated on a series of very popular books about a chicken that flew an airplane. Minnie wrote the text and Willie Faye illustrated the story. Willie Faye married Homer Peet and had twin girls.

Minnie married Ashton Brannock, a captain in the air force who had flown five hundred missions during the war. Ashton was killed in the Korean War, leaving Minnie a young widow with two small children. Minnie went on to write novels for young girls that were adventure survival stories. She eventually remarried and continued to fly into her seventies. In 1993, Minnie was one of several women awarded a Distinguished Service Medal by President Bill Clinton in a White House ceremony. Her mother, Belle Swift, who was 101, attended the ceremony in the Rose Garden.

LIFE IN AMERICA
IN 1932

HISTORICAL NOTE

By the time Herbert Hoover became president in 1929, the bubble of American prosperity had inflated to a size that signified immense wealth. Industry was booming and the stock market was reaching dizzying heights, but no one imagined that a little more than six months after Hoover took office this bubble would burst. The crash came on "Black Tuesday," October 29, 1929. Wall Street panicked and there was a stampede to dump stocks. Stockholders lost forty billion dollars, and the most desperate times in America's history began — the Great Depression. By 1932 banks were closing daily, the lines at soup kitchens were becoming longer and longer, and more Americans than ever were out of work.

The people were so angry about Hoover that his name was used constantly in connection with their misery. The shantytowns that sprang up across the nation were called Hoovervilles. The newspapers that homeless people covered themselves with to stay warm were called Hoover blankets, and people who turned their empty pockets inside out were said to be displaying the Hoover flag. As if the economic situation were not bad enough, the southern plains in western Kansas, Oklahoma, and the Texas Panhandle were suffering the most terrible drought in memory. These once-lush farmlands had been overplanted through the years. Coupled with the drought and the strong winds that began to sweep through in 1931 immense dust storms started to roll across this land, taking not only the precious topsoil but making life nearly impossible. The dust was black. It blotted out the sun and lowered a dark curtain over entire towns. The region became known as the Dust Bowl. Birds were said to fly in terror before the storms, and many animals and people suffocated. Soon there were Dust Bowl refugees, and entire families packed up their belongings in jalopies and headed farther west to California. John Steinbeck, the famous American author, wrote a book about these poverty-stricken Dust Bowl travelers that has become a classic called *The Grapes of Wrath*.

By 1932 one out of every three wage earners

was out of a job — 12.5 million men and women. Malnutrition was also becoming a serious problem among children, and the Manhattan's Children's Bureau reported in 1933 that one out of five American children was not getting enough to eat. A gloom had descended upon the nation, and although Hoover was a man of great integrity the people blamed him. They felt he had done too little too late to help the nation on its slide into abject poverty. New ways were sought and new hope came with the election of New York Governor Franklin Delano Roosevelt as president. At the core of Roosevelt's campaign was what he called a New Deal for America's "forgotten man."

Certain things flourished in these lean times, however: organized crime and entertainment. Famous gangsters and outlaws came to dominate the newspapers. In 1920 a law was passed prohibiting the sale of liquor. This era was known as Prohibition, and gangsters such as Al Capone made a lot of money by bootlegging, the illegal importation and sale of whiskey. But these criminals also were violent men who murdered. Ma Barker was the mother of a gang of outlaws, including her sons, who kidnapped, robbed banks and post offices, and thought nothing of shooting anyone who got in their way. Bonnie Parker and her boyfriend Clyde Barrow went on a violent crime spree of robbery across Texas, Missouri, Oklahoma, and New Mexico before they were finally gunned down in a roadblock ambush. The outlaws fascinated the American reading public, who could not get enough of their exploits and sensational crimes.

But even more engaging than these dark heroes of American crime were the comedians and dramatic characters of the radio. The 1930s were known as the Golden Age of Radio. In 1931 twelve million of America's thirty million homes had a radio, and maybe more than one. Through radio, Americans in their most dire times were brought together and the gloom was dispelled, perhaps through the deadpan humor of one of America's most beloved comics, Jack Benny, or the zany Groucho Marx, or maybe through the popular show *Amos 'n' Andy*, two of America's favorite characters who recounted with outrageous humor their daily misfortunes. In addition to these comedians, there were detective shows such as *Charlie Chan, Sam Spade, Dick Tracy*, and *The Shadow*. And there were science fiction programs like *Buck Rogers in the Twenty-Fifth Century* or *Flash Gordon*. Many of these characters found their way into the comic strips along with Little Orphan Annie and Popeye. The movie industry flourished, for movies were cheap. Clark Gable, Jean Harlow, Gary Cooper, and Greta Garbo with their glamour and beauty provided relief from the dinginess of everyday life during the Depression.

People tried their best to find cheap entertainment, whether it was the movies, listening to radio, roller-skating, which became very popular, and even board games. It was during this time that Monopoly was invented. Despite their heartaches and their despair, Americans were imaginative and resourceful.

Franklin Delano Roosevelt was inaugurated as president in March 1933, and in his stirring inaugural address he gave the people new hope. He spoke his most famous words in that speech when he said, "Let me assert my firm belief that the only thing we have to fear is fear itself — nameless, unreasoning, unjustified terror which paralyzes needed efforts to convert retreat into advance." He went on to say, "Only a foolish optimist can deny the dark realities of the moment."

But he went forward with immediate action. His most urgent problem was the collapse of the banking system. Two days after his inauguration he declared a national holiday in which all banks would be temporarily closed. FDR had drafted an emergency banking bill that was passed a few days later, specifying which banks could reopen. Those allowed to reopen did so with their deposits now insured by the federal government. More safeguards were put in place to protect every single American citizen who put their money in a bank. Over time people's confidence was restored.

In addition to the emergency banking measures that were set up, President Roosevelt started many programs to assist hardship victims, restore jobs, and encourage industrial recovery. He also initiated several laws that were passed pertaining to stock and monetary issues that would guard against future economic crises. Perhaps the most effective programs in FDR's New Deal were the relief programs to relieve unemployment. The Works Progress Administration, or WPA, put to work more than 3.5 million people who had been jobless, building more than half a million miles of roads, 150,000 schools, parks, dams, and other public projects. In addition to construction the WPA sponsored artists and musicians to provide cheap or free recitals, puppet shows, and various classes, as well as public art such as murals and sculpture. Another program, the Civilian Conservation Corps, gave 2.5 million men between the ages of seventeen and twenty-eight jobs planting trees, fighting forest fires, protecting wildlife, building reservoirs, and making trails. Franklin Delano Roosevelt was a man of immense imagination. He also had enormous energy despite being crippled by polio and unable to walk.

FDR's wife, Eleanor, was equally effective and energetic. She was dedicated to bringing women into the mainstream of American politics. She wrote a book called *It's Up to the Women*, which was a call to action for women to lead the way in social justice movements. Eleanor Roosevelt's primary concerns were the abolition of poverty, the end of racial discrimination, and women's rights. She encouraged women to become active in trade unions and consumer rights groups. In 1939 Mrs. Roosevelt joined and became an active member of the National Association for the Advancement of Colored People. She was the most visible first lady in history in terms of the press and the media. She was the first president's wife to give press conferences, and she wrote columns for newspapers and magazines. Perhaps her most famous column, which was regularly published, was called "My Day," in which she wrote about how the Depression affected daily life in the country.

In 1936 Roosevelt was reelected by an overwhelming majority. The New Deal was working and America was gradually lifting itself from the depths of the Depression. It has been said, however, that World War II was as effective as anything in helping the country break loose from the Depression's grip. All of American industry was called into action to produce the arms and supplies needed for war and to stop the dictator Adolf Hitler on his march across Europe.

The Swift family's home, 4605 North Meridian, is based on this house where author Kathryn Lasky's moth *grew up. Built in Indianapolis in 1920 by Lasky's grandparents, Sam and Belle Falender, it housed Sam a* *Belle, as well as Lasky's mother, her four sisters, her brother, and chickens, sheltering them all through Great Depression.*

The radio programs of the 1930s provided relief from the hard times of the Great Depression. There were science fiction shows, comedies, and dramas—quite similar to today's television programs. Jack Benny and Groucho Marx, Buck Rogers and Flash Gordon, Sam Spade and Dick Tracy were just a few of the radio personalities and characters that American listeners loved.

The 1930s are known as the Golden Age of Radio. Approximately 40 percent of all American homes owned at least one radio. Ed Wynn, who was a comic and an actor, starred on a popular radio program as the Texaco Fire Chief. This photograph shows Graham MacNamee and Wynn recording an episode of their show in the National Broadcasting Company's radio studio.

The Circle Theatre in Indianapolis (above), a national historic landmark, was one of the first "deluxe movie palaces" to be built in the midwest. Featuring films with stars such as Clark Gable and Greta Garbo, the movies provided a glamorous escape from the hardships and poverty of the day. Adults and children alike would line up to see romance, comedy, and horror films.

Hollywood's film industry experienced a boom during the 1930s. Indeed, people flocked to the movies because they were inexpensive and entertaining. Greta Garbo, the actress who starred in more than thirty movies and became an icon of the times, influenced the way young women dressed. Berets and cloche hats, sunglasses, and false eyelashes became important elements of ladies' fashion as women tried to mimic Garbo's look.

After the stock market took a dizzying plunge on October 29, 1929, a day known as Black Tuesday, banks and factories began closing down almost daily throughout the nation. By 1932, one-third of the American workforce was out of work. Some wage earners were forced to sell personal belongings on the street, or fruit from their own orchards, to earn a meager living.

Many families had to do their Christmas shopping from outside the store windows during the Depression. Because 12.5 million American men and women were out of work, most luxury items cost too much. As money and essential items were scarce, people could not afford to exchange traditional Christmas presents. Rather, most had to be resourceful and accept that the holiday season would not be the same as it had been in the past.

This ad from December 1932 depicts America's mood at the height of the Great Depression. Readers are encouraged to buy a Christmas tree — even if they cannot afford one — to save themselves from the despair of a holiday season with no brightness in sight.

Soup kitchens opened and bread lines were a common sight. Hunger and malnutrition were becoming serious problems. In this photograph, a line of men wait outside a soup kitchen opened by mobster Al Capone in Chicago, Illinois.

The Girl Scouts, as well as other charitable organizations and individuals, brought baskets of food and Christmas cheer to destitute families living in shantytowns during the holiday season.

Individuals and families who had lost their means of income left their homes behind to squat in these shantytowns that were nicknamed Hoovervilles. President Herbert Hoover received the brunt of the nation's blame for allowing the Great Depression to occur, which continued to worsen Americans' lives at an alarming rate. The occupants of these shantytowns built makeshift homes out of whatever materials were available—tin, wood, tires. Often the homes were not safe for habitation.

While the nation was grappling with the economic ramifications of the Great Depression, the Texas Panhandle, Oklahoma, and the southwestern plains of Kansas were faced with the worst drought in history and strong winds that began blowing in 1931 and lasted most of the decade. The winds swept enormous dust storms across these lands, which were known as the Dust Bowl. Many people fled the area, often heading for California.

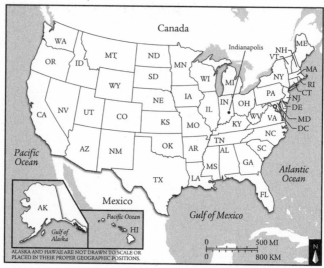

This modern map shows the approximate location of Indianapolis, Indiana.

182

Molasses Crinkles

Ingredients:

3/4 cup shortening

1 cup packed brown sugar

1 egg

1/4 cup molasses

2-1/4 cups all-purpose flour

2 teaspoons baking soda

1/4 teaspoon salt

1/2 teaspoon ground cloves

1 teaspoon ground cinnamon

1 teaspoon ground ginger

1/3 cup granulated sugar for decoration

1. Cream the shortening and the brown sugar. Stir in the egg and molasses and mix well.

2. Combine the flour, baking soda, salt, cloves, cinnamon, and ginger. Add the flour mixture to the shortening mixture and mix well. Cover and chill dough for at least two to three hours.

3. Preheat oven to 350°F (175°C). Grease cookie sheets.

4. Roll dough into balls the size of large walnuts. Roll balls in sugar and place three inches apart on the prepared baking sheets. Bake at 350°F (175°C) for 10 to 12 minutes. Let cool for one minute before transferring to a wire rack to continue cooling.

Makes 3–4 dozen.

Molasses Crinkles were a popular dessert during the Depression and today.

ABOUT THE AUTHOR

Kathryn Lasky says that of all the Dear America books she has written, this is her favorite and the most personal. Indeed, she took the experiences of her own mother's family growing up in Indianapolis during the Depression as the basis of her story.

The house of the Swift family at 4605 North Meridian was indeed built by Kathryn's grandparents Sam and Belle Falender in 1920 to house their lively brood of five girls and one boy. Minnie, Clementine, Adelaide, and Gwen are modeled after Kathryn Lasky's own aunts, and Ozzie is modeled after her uncle. Kathryn decided that having to deal with five girls in one book was just too many, so she made the four Swift girls composites of her aunts and her mother.

The furnishings described in the house, the rooms, and even the chickens are all true to the way the house was when the Falenders lived in it. Kathryn Lasky says, "I never saw the house during the Depression, for I wasn't born then. But I do remember going there when I was a toddler in the forties. I remember Jackie and the chickens. I remember my mother showing me the sleeping porch where they slept for almost half the year, and I remember the sunporch with its lovely hand-painted murals of fruit and flowers."

Kathryn Lasky also remembers her parents talking about the radio shows from that era and the movies, two for a dime, downtown. Lasky herself as a little girl was taken to Ayres tearoom for lunch and loved the chicken à la king.

Ms. Lasky says she has memories of all her aunts, but the most vivid are of her aunt Mildy, after whom Lady is modeled. "Aunt Mildy was kind of wild," Lasky says. Clementine most resembles Lasky's mother, Hortense, who did become a social worker and marry a man named Marven Lasky. Like Marlon he came from Minnesota and was terribly handsome and funny and smart. Lasky wrote about her father in another book called *Marven of the Great North Woods*, which won the National Jewish Book Award. And she earlier wrote about her father's family's escape from tzarist Russia in the book *The Night Journey*.

Kathryn Lasky has received many awards for her writing, including the Newbery Honor, the Boston Globe – Horn Book Award, and the *Washington Post* Children's Book Guild Award for Nonfiction. She lives in Cambridge, Massachusetts, with her husband, Christopher Knight. They have two grown children.

Ms. Lasky is the author of more than thirty books for children and adults, including, most recently, the Guardians of Ga'Hoole and the Wolves of the Beyond series, as well as the Daughters of the Sea books. She won a Newbery Honor for her book *Sugaring Time*, a National Jewish Book Award for *The Night Journey*, and the *Washington Post* Children's Book Guild Award for her contribution to children's nonfiction. She has also written several Dear America diaries, in addition to two historical fiction books — *Beyond the Burning Time*, an ALA Best Book for Young Adults, and *True North* — for Scholastic. She lives in Cambridge, Massachusetts, with her family.

ACKNOWLEDGMENTS

Grateful acknowledgment is made for permission to use the following:

Cover portrait by Tim O'Brien.

Cover background: The Granger Collection.

Page 174: The Falender house, photograph by Marsh Davis, courtesy of Indiana Landmarks.

Page 175 (top): Children listening to the radio, Superstock.

Page 175 (bottom): Ed Wynn (left), Culver Pictures.

Page 176 (top): Circle Theatre, Bass Photo, Neg. #218620F, Indiana Historical Society.

Page 176 (bottom): Lining up for the movies, Brown Brothers.

Page 177: Greta Garbo, ibid.

Page 178: Apple stand, Archive Photos/Getty Images.

Page 179 (top): Window shopping, Brown Brothers.

Page 179 (bottom): Christmas shopping ad, Indiana State Archives, Indiana Commission on Public Records.

Page 180 (top): Soup kitchen, Archive Photos/ Getty Images.

Page 180 (bottom): Girl Scouts, Indiana State Archives, Indiana Commission on Public Records.

Page 181 (top): Shantytown, Culver Pictures.

Page 181 (bottom): Shantytown men, Archive Photos/Getty Images.

Page 182 (top): Dust Bowl, SSPL/Getty Images.

Page 182 (bottom): Map by Heather Saunders.

OTHER BOOKS IN THE DEAR AMERICA SERIES

DEAR AMERICA

The Diary of Emma Simpson

When Will This Cruel War Be Over?

Gordonsville, Virginia, 1864

BARRY DENENBERG

DEAR AMERICA

The Diary of Deliverance Trembley, Witness to the Salem Witch Trials

I Walk in Dread

Massachusetts Bay Colony, 1691

LISA ROWE FRAUSTINO

DEAR AMERICA

The Diary of Hattie Campbell

Across the Wide and Lonesome Prairie

The Oregon Trail, 1847

KRISTIANA GREGORY

DEAR AMERICA

The Diary of Abigail Jane Stewart

The Winter of Red Snow

Valley Forge, Pennsylvania, 1777

KRISTIANA GREGORY

DEAR AMERICA

The Second Diary of Abigail Jane Stewart

Cannons at Dawn

Valley Forge, Pennsylvania, 1779

KRISTIANA GREGORY

DEAR AMERICA

The Diary of Patsy, a Freed Girl

I Thought My Soul Would Rise and Fly

Mars Bluff, South Carolina, 1865

JOYCE HANSEN

DEAR AMERICA

The Diary of Amelia Martin

A Light in the Storm

Fenwick Island, Delaware, 18

KAREN HESSE

DEAR AMERICA

The Diary of Piper Davis

The Fences Between Us

Seattle, Washington, 1941

KIRBY LARSON

DEAR AMERICA

The Diary of Remember Patience Whipple

A Journey to the New World

Mayflower, 1620

KATHRYN LASKY

DEAR AMERICA

The Diary of Lydia Amelia Pierce

LIKE THE WILLOW TREE

Portland, Maine, 1918

LOIS LOWRY

DEAR AMERICA

The Diary of Clotee, a Slave

A Picture of Freedom

Belmont Plantation, Virginia,

PATRICIA C. McKISSA

DEAR AMERICA

The Diary of Catherine Carey Logan

Standing in the Light

Delaware Valley, Pennsylvania, 1763

MARY POPE OSBORNE

DEAR AMERICA

The Diary of Angeline Reddy

Behind the Masks

Bodie, California, 1880

SUSAN PATRON

DEAR AMERICA

The Diary of Dawnie Rae Johnson

With the Might of Angels

Hadley, Virginia, 1954

ANDREA DAVIS PINKNEY

DEAR AMERICA

The Diary of Margaret Ann Ro

Voyage on the Great Titanic

RMS Titanic, 1912

ELLEN EMERSON WHI